I STAYED

TOO LONG...

A Novel

Jan Davis

I Stayed Too Long by Jan Davis
Copyright © 2015 by Jan Davis
Published by She Pours Publishing
LIBRARY OF CONGRESS CATALOG IN PUBLICATION

ISBN-13: 9780578174181

Printed December 2015
Printed in the United States of America

SHE POURS PUBLISHING
"POURING OUT WITH PEN AS HE POURS IN"
www.shepourspublishing.com

I Stayed Too Long...

Jan Davis

Dedication

This book is dedicated to the most phenomenal woman of God I've ever known: my mother, Barbara Jean Meriweather. Thank you for being an amazing example of integrity, perseverance, love and sacrifice. You have most certainly established a godly legacy in the earth that will continue to bless generations long after you've been promoted on to Glory. I honor and love you fiercely.

Acknowledgments

To my incredible husband: Mr. Brian Keith Davis. Never have I met a man with a heart like yours! I love you completely and exclusively. Thank you for the healing you've brought to me and our family.

To our phenomenal children, Regina and son-in-law Steven, Reginald II, Ryan, Robin, Jared, and Gabrielle, you make being a mother a joy! You have been a constant source of encouragement during this project… can't say thank you enough. Stay determined to live your lives in a manner that honors God and leave a godly legacy. Your lives will continue to speak long after you pass away, make sure it speaks well.

To my absolutely amazing grandchildren, Roydrick, Rhyane, Savion, Reginald III, Xavier, Jacob, Rashaun, Keion, Jordan, and Zohri there is greatness in you! Serve God with your lives! Granjan loves you fiercely!!

To my awesome brother's Floyd, Guan, and the late Frankie and Charles Meriweather, and beautiful sister's, Robin, Lisa, Tracy, the late Denise Benford, Beverly and Doris, there are no greater siblings on the earth! Thanks for your love and encouragement.

To Aunt Peppie & Uncle Tommy, Aunt Judy, Aunt Debbie, and Uncle Van thank you for your prayers and all you've poured into me! In honor of my late Uncles, Cornell (my favorite), Bradford Sr. miss you, and Jeffrey.

My beautiful Nieces, Tamala, Brittany, Courtney, Megan, Ronesha, Penny, Courtney and Shanise, my amazing Nephews, Kevin, Brandon, Bryan, the late

Christopher, Connor, Caleb, Croix, Tony, and Keith; looking forward to seeing all the great things God has for your lives come into fruition. Crazy in love with you all!

My great nieces, nephews and cousins, you're all so very close to my heart. Pursue Him and His purpose for your lives!

To our extended children, Tamika, Jaron and Tiffany, Lamont, Doug, Sesen, Timeka, Ashanti, Iesha, Marquita (thank you!), Jessica and Jason, Christina, LaRonda, Ron, Corey, Jimmy, Lewis and Ray and Marquita, you know you're in my heart and prayers, there is greatness in you! To Sarissa, Glam-ma adores you.

To my Senior Pastor's, Brett and Gizelle and Scott and Melanie Jones, your wisdom and humility amaze me, I honor you all! Thank you for your sacrifice. Pastors Keith Cistrunk and his lovely wife Dana, your leadership and compassion bless us all. Bishop Shelton Bady, thank you for teaching me excellence, order, and submission. Pastor Calvin and Trina Jackson of Rebirth Believers Fellowship, Pastor's truly after God's heart. Your passion for the maturation of the Body of Christ and love for people are life changing.

To my spiritual Mothers and Mentors, Elder Althea Bacchus, Apostle Joyce James, Mrs. Rose Falls and her wonderful husband Bruce, Pastor Carolyn Cofield, and Pastor Belinda Barber, all General's in the Body of Christ. Thank you for being my Elijah's and allowing me to be your Elisha! Your prayers and example have changed the very trajectory of my life. I am forever grateful, I love and honor you all.

I also honor Pastor Pastor Elaine Benson, Prophetess Briggie Stansberry, and Dr. Henri Williams, thank you for unselfishly pouring into me and countless others, our lives are better because of your "Yes" to the Lord.

To my Sister/Friends, Eva Johnson and Terry Theall - Jones, my best friends for the past 20+ years! Maceo and Stacey Joseph-Harris, Marolda Cameron, Daphanie Travis, and Loyce Karari, you ladies are fierce!! God has highly favored me with you! Thank you all for praying with and for me…and for those "interventions." Ha!

Kim McQuitty, Sanford & Karen Robinson, Pastor's Mike and Latasha Rugemer, Evangelist Shandra Powell, Constance Darby, Shelia Benard, Pertrice Ross, Joann Norman, Debra Riley, Mary Wheatfall, Bradford and Sonja Lowe, James & Nicole White, Mike and Kristi Wall, Michael and Danielle Ward, Ron & Charlotte Stallings, Theo and Margo Hickman, Jackie Rudison, Jacqui Hill, and Vickie Ochiche, what a tremendous blessing and privilege it has been doing life and ministry with you!!!

To the "Elijah's:" Maranda, Herlinda, April, Asha, Ashanti, Crystal, Fran, Iesha, Latarrie, Philicia, Tyesha, Quenneisa, Marquita, Danielle, Tracy, Jessica, Kim, and, Bridgette, thank you for allowing me to be your Elijah. I pray a double portion on your lives as you follow hard after God! You're forever in my heart. To Camille Benard, thank you for the inspiration!

The entire Grace Church of Humble Women's LDC, love learning from you and sharing with you!! To Mrs. Regina, Ms. Andre and Mrs. Goldeen, you ladies rock!!!

To Ramsey & Janaia Pratt of "Impressions by Pratt," an absolute Picasso with the camera and graphic design!!! Thank you!!!

To Keba Bacchus of *"Face to Face,"* your artistry with cosmetics is nothing short of amazing!!! Thank you!!!

To Dawnyelle Bacon, an incredible Mom with incredible kids, Tauryn, Taylon. To the G Team, you make work a pleasure! To Karen Brown…Thank you!

Introducing... Janet Davis

My name is Janet Meriweather-Davis. I was born and raised in St. Louis, Missouri and now live in Houston, Texas. I am married to the most wonderful and honorable man I've ever known, Brian K. Davis, whom I absolutely respect and adore.

Together we have six beautiful children and to date, ten phenomenal grandchildren.

I received my Minister's license in 1994. My only qualifications for ministry were simply that I had been molested. I was very promiscuous. I was a pregnant teen. I've had abortions. I have been an adulterer and I've looked for love in all the wrong places. Through nothing but the amazing love and grace of God, I am saved, healed, delivered and growing in Him daily.

I have been forgiven and had to forgive. I have had the honor of sitting with a recovering drug addict until sunrise, when she was strong enough to face another day. I've held mother that lost her only child at the hands of her abusive husband until she cried herself to sleep. I've cried myself to sleep after speaking with a 13yr old young lady who had been abused and neglected since birth and now faced murder charges for killing one of her abusers.

I pray this book brings healing and encouragement to forgive, but most of all, a realization of the amazing relentless love and transforming power of God. I pray abusers that recognize themselves in the pages of this book, acknowledge that fact and immediately seek help. I pray those who are being abused will have the courage to find a way out. There is help, there is hope in God. Please, please, don't stay too long.

Blessings,

JAN

PROLOGUE

"Oh God...how did I get here?" The blood rushing from my body felt strangely warm against my cold skin. *Is this it? Is this the end?'* I thought as I heard the sirens in the distance. *'Are they coming for me?'*

How did all this happen? How could I have let this happen? Where was I when my life began to spiral out of control? What was I thinking? "Lord, please help me. Please..."

I can remember...I remember...the day. The beginning of it all...

Jan Davis

CHAPTER 1

"**A**ngel, come in, it's time for dinner," Momma called from the front porch of our modest, three bedroom, ranch style home in Springfield, Missouri.

Across the street from my house in Wilson Park, stood a beautiful, majestic old oak tree. When I climbed that tree I felt like I could see the whole world. I loved to hear the sound of the wind gently blowing through the brilliantly colored autumn leaves.

In my tree I shared my ten year old deepest thoughts and grandest dreams. I could hide and cry there. Its leaves shielded me from all that was bad in the world. In my tree I was invisible. It was one of only two places where I felt safe. The other was at the church, where me, Momma and my little brother, Alex, attended faithfully.

As a child, I loved New Hope Church. The harmony of the acapella singing was amazing. With no instruments, all we had to keep rhythm was Sister Murphy beating her tambourine like it stole something, while everyone else tapped their feet on the old wooden floor. Most of all, I loved seeing God move through Pastor Carroll's sermons.

Miracles happened in that place as the older women prayed. I believe their prayers literally shook heaven. Even at a young age, I understood the wisdom in the lines on their faces – oh how they loved God.

One Sunday morning, I was sitting in the seat next to a lady well into her eighties who stood to give her testimony. She was frail and bent over and shared how glad she was to be in the house of the Lord. She spoke of how she longed to see the face of her loving Savior and behold the beauty of Heaven. With her eyes closed she smiled as she shared how she would bow before the very throne of God and worship at His feet, when all of a sudden, in a flash, she was no longer bent over.

It was like she was standing at attention. Then I saw the most amazing thing – her spirit came through the top of her head as her body emptied and fell to the floor. Suddenly a massive, beautiful angel ushered her right through the ceiling of the church and no doubt straight to Heaven.

Momma and the others ran to help her, but I knew at that exact moment she was experiencing the very thing she had just testified. They immediately called for an ambulance, but she was already gone. Her life on earth had served its purpose and now she was being promoted into Heaven. It was a beautiful, peaceful, experience and for some reason I had absolutely no fear. It was a day I will never forget it.

New Hope and my tree were my safe havens. I

would sing the songs I learned at church in my tree and be anything I imagined. I could be a doctor curing dreadful diseases. I could be a teacher who loved her students, especially those who were bullied or not so popular. But my favorite was a beautiful princess waiting for my prince to rescue me from..."Angel, come on now, dinner's on the table!" Momma yelled a second time.

As I made my way down my tree, I saw him pull into the driveway. I swallowed hard and thought about climbing right back up my tree. I watched as he got out of the car. *'Is he good daddy today or bad daddy,'* I thought to myself? My heart pounded and I could actually taste the fear.

As he stumbled up the walkway, Momma watched him intensely. I believe she tasted the same fear. He stopped halfway up the walkway, pointed his finger at Momma and began too curse and yell. I hurried down the tree and ran across the street. I was so scared for my Momma. *'He's bad daddy.'*

"Hey daddy, glad you're home," I tried to distract him.

"Where the hell you been girl?" he said cutting his eyes at me.

"I was just across the street at the park daddy – playing."

"Get your ugly, useless self in the house!"

"Yes sir daddy, I'm sorry daddy," I said trembling. Cautiously, I walked passed him making sure to stay out of arms reach.

Momma grabbed my hand and ushered me quickly into the house. "Go in your room Angel, and don't come out. I'll bring your dinner in to you later." I wondered why or what I did to make him hate me so much.

My little brother Alex was sitting in the living room watching TV. We made eye contact as I hurried into my room. Instantly, he recognized the fear and knew tonight he was *"bad daddy."*

Alex jumped up, turned off the television and stood at attention. "Hi daddy," he said forcing a smile.

"Come over here my boy and give your daddy a big hug!" Alex quickly ran over and hugged him. "You're daddy's big, little man. You're gonna be just like me when you grow up."

"God, I sure hope not," I said under my breath as I peeked out the door of my room.

Without any warning, he turned his attention and rage back to Momma. "What's this crap you got on my table?"

"John, it's good, just taste it. I made it especially for you," Momma said trying to appease him.

Daddy walked to the table and picked up the glass of lemonade. He smelled it, looked at Momma, then with a sadistic twisted grin on his face, walked over to her and poured the whole glass of lemonade over her head. Then threw it into the wall where it shattered into a million pieces. Shards of glass flew everywhere.

When I saw Momma bleeding, I ran from my room into the bathroom grabbed a wet towel and rushed to her aid. She looked at me with terror in her eyes and commanded me back to my room. She grabbed Alex, and I and pushed us into the room and closed the door.

We ran into the closet, our usual hiding place. I covered Alex's ears, but we could still hear all the horrible names he called her. We heard every slap and punch. Not to mention the dishes breaking as they crashed to the floor. Momma's screaming, crying and begging him to stop was terrifying. Suddenly the doorbell rang and everything went silent. I didn't know who it was, but I was so very grateful for their timing.

Alex and I ventured from our hiding place and opened the bedroom door to see who our savior was. "Who the hell is it?!"

"It's Mr. Lucas, from next door."

"Hey Lucas, what do you want?" Bad daddy growled as he opened the door.

"Well, how are you John? How are Donna and the kids? I thought I heard a little ruckus, so I..."

"They're fine. Everything is fine, we just about to sit down to dinner. Thanks for stopping by Lucas," he slammed the door.

Bad daddy looked at Momma with total disgust and said, "Clean this mess up and clean yourself up. You ain't worth a dime. You look like you've been hit by a train," he walked into their bedroom and slammed the door. We could hear him laughing as if beating Momma and terrorizing us was somehow entertaining.

Alex cried for Momma as I helped tend to her wounds. As usual, she told us everything was going to be alright and that she was fine, but her split lip, black eye, and swollen jaw said differently. I'm not sure who she was trying to convince, us or herself. She winced and held her side every time she breathed. It was obvious that he had kicked her, and he was still wearing his work boots.

I remember vividly, when I was about four years old, trying to console her as she cried from one of her numerous beatings. Just then, I realized something – this time I wasn't crying. On that day I made the decision to never, ever, let that happen to me. If that was love, I didn't want anything to do with it. Right there at that very moment the first brick of the wall I'd spend years skillfully building around my heart was laid. I decided never to cry or let anyone hurt me again – especially my daddy.

———— ❊ ————

Momma, what a wonderful godly woman. She had long, silky, coal black hair and her skin was dark brown, smooth as the finest chocolate. Her eyes were hazel and changed from a light brown to greenish brown. I'm not sure what triggered the color change, but Grandmamma used to say it was her mood. She was a full figured woman with perfect posture. She was a very beautiful woman before the years of stress, depression and abuse took their toll.

Every morning I'd wake up to her sitting by the radio with her Bible, pen and notebook listening to the preachers as they ministered. Momma loved the Word of

God. Bad daddy wasn't a problem on Sunday mornings. He had to sleep off the Friday and Saturday night drinking binges.

On Saturday nights Momma would set out everything we needed, from her clothes and shoes to the ribbons for my hair. Even though daddy slept hard she didn't risk waking him by making multiple trips into their bedroom.

My momma came from a long line of praying women. My Grandmamma was a sweet little round woman, very quiet and accommodating. She could sew, knit and grew the prettiest mums, roses and tulips in her garden. Unfortunately, she died when I was three years old. Momma was a great cook, Alex and I salivated as we smelled her famous fried chicken from down the street.

Momma had one brother, Uncle Keith. He was in the Air Force and stationed overseas. He would often call, but we rarely got to see him. Momma never told him about the fights between her and bad daddy. She said there was no point in worrying him. After all, what could he do? He was thousands of miles away.

Momma was always sacrificing for me and Alex and made do with very little. Daddy made good money, but we rarely saw the benefits. He would literally gamble away thousands of dollars. The phone, lights or gas were always getting turned off.

John/daddy was a very tall, handsome man with deep dimples, beautiful dark brown eyes, weathered caramel skin and a bald head. I knew very little about his family or how he grew up. Momma told me he was born and raised in Mississippi. His mother was African American,

White and American Indian. She died years before I was born, but from the pictures I saw she was beautiful, but her eyes looked sad.

I never heard him talk about his father and we never saw any pictures with him and his parents. His other brothers all lived in the nearby suburbs, but we had never met them and daddy had no contact with them. Something must have happened to tear their family apart. I often wondered what landed him on the path to becoming an abusive alcoholic. What pain was he trying to escape? What shame was he trying to mask?

Everybody has a story – I wish I knew his. Maybe it would help make some sense out of why he was the way he was and why he hated me and Momma so much. I concluded it had to be me. If I could only be good enough, pretty enough or smart enough, maybe he would love me. Maybe he would love us.

CHAPTER 2

Alex and I were in the living room watching our Saturday morning cartoons when we heard a car pull into the driveway. It was Sister Melvena Johnson from church. We loved Sister Johnson. She was rather loud and had a contagious laugh. When she walked everything bounced. Momma always said we had to speak louder when Sister Johnson came over because she was a little hard of hearing.

She got out of her brand new 1969 shiny blue Cadillac, adjusted her wig, (which somehow always managed to turn sideways), tugged at her skirt, then made sure her knee high support hose weren't showing. Once her ensemble was perfect, she began her jolly stroll up the walkway. "Momma, Sister Johnson is here!" We yelled.

Momma quickly ran from the kitchen to her bedroom to mask her battle scars with makeup. Before Sister Johnson could ring the doorbell I opened the door. "Well, hello my Dears," she said pulling us into her ample bosom.

Sister Johnson always made us feel special. "Good Morning Sister Johnson," Alex and I said in complete harmony. "How are you?"

"Oh, I'm right fine – right fine my darlings. Is your mother up or am I too early?"

"Oh, no Ma'am, Momma will be right out."

"Now you know I have something for my darlings," she said reaching into her purse and pulled out chocolates filled with caramel.

"Thank you so much Sister Johnson!" We cheered we grabbed as many chocolates as our small hands could hold.

"Now make sure you ask your mother before you eat those. And don't eat too many – don't want you getting a tummy ache."

"Yes Ma'am."

We could hear Momma talking to daddy in their bedroom. Although we couldn't make out what they were saying, I could tell he was agitated. Sister Johnson was the only person daddy seemed to fear. She had a way of looking at him that dared him to disrespect her. Momma and I marveled at how she handled him.

As I tried to discern their conversation, Sister Johnson interrupted the silence. "So, have you two been keeping busy? How's school coming along? You know you gotta work hard and get good grades."

"Yes Ma'am," Alex and I chimed.

The voices stopped, the door opened and Momma made her way down the hallway. "Well, hello Sister Johnson," she greeted.

Sister Johnsons' face grimaced at the sight of Momma. "Hello Sister Donna, so good to see you my dear," She said quickly changing her expression.

"My Darlings, will you do Sister Johnson a big favor? Will you please go and play while your mother and I talk?"

"Yes Ma'am," we said as made our exit.

I followed Alex into his room and pulled some of his favorite toys out to play. As soon as he was settled I went into my room so I could hear Momma and Sister Johnson talking. "He did it again, didn't he?" Sister Johnson asked angrily.

"He doesn't mean to. I gotta try harder not to push his buttons."

"Oh, I'll push his buttons alright!" Sister Johnson said pushing Momma aside as she marched down the hall towards their room.

"Sister Johnson, please, please don't go in there. Just let him sleep it off. Everything is fine," Momma said as she ran after her.

Sister Johnson stopped after she passed my room. Momma quickly ushered her back into the living room. "Donna, that man had no right putting his hands on you! Oh, my – look at your face. Why, do you keep letting him do this to you?!"

"You don't understand – he's been through a lot.

He's a hard worker and really does love me and the kids. He just doesn't know how to express his feelings."

"Oh, he doesn't have any trouble expressing his feelings – look at your face Donna. Can't you see? That man's gonna kill you one day!"

"We've been married twelve years. The first year was pretty good, but every year it seems to get worse. He may hit me, but he would never hurt me bad enough to kill me. I've just got to find a way to show him I love him and he'll be okay. I'm praying for him every day."

"I'm glad you're praying for him baby, but he's gotta want to change. I'm not saying divorce him, but get out while you still can Donna. The last two beatings put you in the hospital with broken ribs and two broken fingers, remember?"

"We're going to be just fine, you'll see. Now, what brought you by today?"

"I just wanted to let you know that I'm moving to North Carolina to take care of my mother. She fell and broke her hip, bless her heart. She can't take care of herself anymore, so I've got to be there for her. But Donna, I sure hate to leave you and them darlings."

As I closed the door I thought about everything Sister Johnson said to Momma. Although I hated seeing what he does to her, where would we go? Uncle Keith was overseas and now Sister Johnson was moving. Maybe Momma's right. Maybe we've just got to find a way to love daddy better. Make him happy. I know it's me messing things up for her. If I wasn't here, maybe Momma, daddy and Alex could be a happy family.

"I hate you!" I said looking at my reflection in the mirror.

CHAPTER 3

Uncle Donny wasn't really my uncle, but a friend of my daddy's. Many of our neighbors were having beautiful patio decks added to their homes. Daddy really liked them and wanted to have one added to our house, so he decided to do it himself and asked Uncle Donny to help. Alex was so excited and gladly accepted the title of "daddy's little helper."

Momma and I were in the kitchen preparing lunch for the work crew of three – tuna fish sandwiches, chips and Momma's famous lemonade. After lunch daddy discovered he needed more nails and decided he didn't like the color of the wood stain he'd chosen, so he and Uncle Donny would go to the hardware store. Uncle Donny declined, saying he would stay and cut the wooden planks to size.

Since daddy had to go to the store, Momma thought it would be a good time to wash Alex up and put him down for a nap. We had finished the dishes, so she let me go outside to play. While I was playing Uncle Donny called me over and asked where daddy kept his tools. He needed some kind of what-cha-ma-call-it to do something or another.

I told him that daddy's tools were in the basement. He went to the basement and called me again saying he couldn't find them and asked me to show him where they were. So I made my way down the stairs and showed Uncle Donny daddy's arsenal of tools.

Uncle Donny touched my hair and told me how soft it was and asked if I'd like to hear a story. I wanted to go outside and climb my tree, but he insisted on telling me his story. With Momma upstairs tending to Alex and daddy gone to the hardware store, it was a perfect time for him to *"tell me his story."*

Our basement was daddy's "man cave." The paneled walls were covered with his favorite football team's posters and banners. The console TV, which was his prize possession, stood in the corner and the brown leather furniture was strategically placed around it. Uncle Donny sat in daddy's favorite chair and placed me on his lap. While telling me a story about a beautiful princess, he began to rub my hair, then my back and thighs.

I thought he had something in his pocket because suddenly it felt like I was sitting on something rather hard. He continued his story saying, "If you really love someone you have to show you love them." Then he asked if I loved him. "Sure Uncle Donny, I love you."

Uncle Donny put his hands under my shirt as he tickled me. "Good because I love you too. Can I show you how I love you?"

"Oh, yes!" I said willingly. *'Finally, someone loves me,'* I thought innocently.

Uncle Donny's put his hands into my pants. He told me when you love someone you have to keep their secrets. He said if I told our secret he wouldn't love me anymore and that something bad would happen to me. So I kept his secret, because more than anything, I wanted to be loved.

As Uncle Donny got closer to our family he started taking me and Alex to the movies and other special places. Afterwards he would always take us back to his house, put Alex down for a nap or let him watch cartoons, and then show me how much he loved me. He loved me until I was ten years old.

As I got older I often thought about why I kept his secret. I guess at the time I actually thought it was love. Though I wondered why it had to be a secret, I never considered it abuse. I never felt physical pain because there was never penetration. It was mostly fondling and him masturbating in front of me. Every time daddy abused Momma, he not only hurt her, he hurt us. There was always physical pain with daddy, but not with Uncle Donny.

Suddenly, Uncle Donny just stopped coming around. I thought it was something I did wrong. Maybe daddy was right, I was worthless. From time to time Alex would ask about him, but I never did.

CHAPTER 4

Just before the long awaited Christmas break, the weather was cold and crisp. Momma bundled us up like we were going to Siberia. Long underwear, corduroy pants, wool sweaters, jacket, coats, hats, scarves and gloves. As if that wasn't enough, she got a big dollop of petroleum jelly and smeared it all over our faces. We shined like new coins. But I have to admit, it did provide great protection against the sharp cold winter wind.

There were no school buses in our neighborhood, so we had to walk. It was about a good mile to Harriston Elementary School, so we were grateful for the bundling. We had a car, but daddy had to be to work early and wouldn't allow Momma to take him, so she could keep the car.

I liked school, but I never seemed to fit in with the girls because I was such a tom-boy. I loved climbing trees, playing baseball and racing the boys and was faster than a lot of them. The girls wore pretty bows in their hair, but I was satisfied with my long ponytail. Momma would press my hair and curl it, but a few hours later I'd pull it right back into a ponytail.

The boys accepted me – I was one of them. I was twelve years old and in the seventh grade, so other than my ponytail, I looked a lot like them too. My attire was sweat shirts and corduroy pants in the winter and tee shirts and blue jeans in the summer – with the exception of Sundays of course.

Sunday's attire consisted of frilly freshly ironed, starched cotton dresses and black patent leather shoes. I have to admit, I liked dressing up. That's when Momma told me how pretty I looked and Alex how handsome he was.

After I walked Alex to his Kindergarten class; I headed to building "B," which housed the Junior High students. Just as I hung up my coat, in walked my nightmares, Rosie Gillard and Marla Harvey. Rosie had transferred to our school the previous year. She was from what I considered one of the "tough schools," Gunhaden Elementary. She was taller than most of the girls in Junior High and a master at using her height and the fact that she attended Gunhaden to intimidate us.

Marla was her short stocky sidekick, whom I had known since first grade. She always seemed to have a runny nose, even in the summer. Rosie's purpose in life was to make mine miserable and she did a great job of it. Just the sound of her voice struck a chord of fear within me. "Look at Angel – where did you get those pants from, the Goodwill?"

The class erupted in laughter as I tried to pretend I

didn't hear her comment. "You heard her!" Marla chimed.

I picked up my books and headed for my seat, never acknowledging either of them. Rosie followed behind me and pushed me so hard my books flew out of my hands and I went tumbling over my desk onto the floor. Just then, Mrs. Hammerly walked in the room. "What in the world are you doing Angel!" she scolded.

Rosie extended her hand to help me up. "I told Angel not to stand on her desk or she might fall Mrs. Hammerly," She said with the most innocent look as she pulled me to my feet.

"So you were standing on the desk, were you young lady?"

"No, Mrs. Hammerly, Rosie pushed me," I tried to explain.

"Stop that lying! Why on earth your mother named you "Angel" is beyond me. Now, take this note and go to the Principal's office. I'll not have this foolishness in my classroom."

Rosie had a devilish smirk on her face as she watched me pick up my books and take the note. Three days suspension was my sentence. I was given a white sealed envelope with "Mrs. Donna Sanders," written in angry big red letters. I had to sit on the bench outside the Principal's office all day and wasn't even allowed to have lunch.

My biggest fear was what daddy would say or do. The three o'clock bell rang and students gathered in the halls. I was released, but waited to make sure everyone left before I went back into the class room. When the coast was clear, I grabbed my coat and hurried to pick up Alex. That's when I overheard some of the kids saying Rosie was looking for me.

Alex and I ducked back into the building. I went into the girl's bathroom with him in tow to wait until the coast was clear. "Yuck, this is the girl's bathroom!" Alex protested.

"Quiet Alex, do you want them to find us?" We waited in the silence for ten minutes or so and then I peeked out to make sure the halls were clear. Once the coast was clear I took Alex by the hand and started on the cold journey home.

As we walked all I could think about giving that letter to my momma. Tears tried to come, but I commanded them to dry up. What good would it do? I was training myself not to feel, to be numb and was becoming very good at it.

Momma greeted us at the door. Even though I dreaded giving her the letter I was glad to be home before daddy arrived. I wanted to make sure I gave it to her before he got home. I began explaining what happened as I unbundled. When I handed her the letter, she opened it and read it aloud.

"Angel was very disruptive in Mrs. Hammerly's class today. She stood on the top of her desk which caused it to fall over, endangering herself and other students. She is therefore suspended for the next three days and we are requesting a parent/teacher meeting upon her return."

"Angel, you have to do better. What am I gonna tell your daddy?"

"Do we have to tell him?"

"Just get to your homework, I'll figure something out."

By the time daddy came home Alex and I were asleep. We were awakened by the terrifying sound of him yelling at Momma. "So, why didn't you tell me that stupid girl got suspended from school? I'm gonna teach you about hiding stuff from me. Why you trying to cover for her anyway, she ain't ever gonna be any good. She's worthless just like you!"

Alex ran to my room and hopped in my bed trembling and crying. Evidently, bad daddy found the letter before Momma had a chance to tell him about it. I didn't know what to do. It was all my fault.

I told Alex to hide in the closet as I opened the door and ran into the living room. Momma was on the floor covering her face trying to protect herself from another blow. "Daddy, daddy, I'm sorry, it's my fault!!! I asked Momma not to tell you 'cause I didn't want to get in trouble."

Bad daddy slowly turned and looked at me with his eyes full of hate. I wished I could have disappeared. "Get over here right now!!!"

"Yes, sir," I said slowly making my way across the room. He slapped me so hard I could taste the blood in my mouth before I hit the floor.

Like Momma, I covered my face to shield myself

from the next blow. "Get up!!!" he said kicking me in my back.

"Stop!!!" Momma ran over to shield me.

Alex ran out of the bedroom crying and begging him not to hit us again. When he saw the fear on Alex's face, he cursed, walked into the bathroom and slammed the door. Momma grabbed me crying and saying how sorry she was, but I didn't shed a tear. After his beating I got up, wiped my mouth with the sleeve of my pajamas and got back into bed.

For the first time I felt a hardness: I felt hate. I wished he would go away and never come back. Even though I hated daddy, I longed for his love at the same time.

Embracing hatred, I lay numb and told myself, *'I should have been hurt - that I deserved it – I'm a horrible girl – nothing I do is right.'* I blamed myself for every beating Momma suffered. It was all my fault. That night I drifted off to sleep – no tears.

There were many incidents in our childhood where I remember wishing Mr. Lucas, our next door neighbor, was our father and this was one of them. Mr. Lucas had two daughters, Ava and Alma. When Mrs. Lucas would invite me and Alex over for fresh baked cookies, I used to study Ava and Alma. The way they talked and how they behaved.

I thought since their daddy loved them, maybe my daddy would love me too if I acted like they did. I wanted to be anybody but who I was. I ached for his love, affirmation and approval, but it never came, so I just ached.

CHAPTER 5

The summer was quickly coming to an end and even though I had a terrible time in school, Momma said something about this year was going to be different. The 8th grade would be a special time for me. It was my last year in Junior High School. Momma had been telling me for nearly a week that she had a big surprise for me. I begged her to tell me, but she wouldn't budge. She always loved surprising us.

Friday morning, the last weekend before school started I heard a car pull into our driveway. I pulled open the curtains covering the large picture window in the living room and to my surprise, it was Sister Johnson! As fast as my feet could carry me I ran out to meet her with Alex close behind. Sister Johnson flung the car door open and hurried to meet us. "Oh my goodness, look at you two. Alex, I believe you've grown a foot since I last laid eyes on you and look how handsome you are."

"Angel, you are just as pretty as a picture. What a beautiful young lady you are."

Sister Johnson came back to town for a visit and she and Momma were taking me school shopping. They both agreed it was time for me to change my tom-boy attire. Momma was determined to turn me into a young lady. For the first time in a long time I had something to be excited about. "What a wonderful surprise!" I said hugging Momma tightly as I thanked her over and over again for loving me.

That was one of the best days of my life, I remember like it was yesterday. It was the only time Momma had ever taken me school shopping. Normally, she just ordered what she could afford out of a catalog and had it delivered to the house. Since daddy never let her drive I guess it was easier. Thank God for good ole Sister Johnson and her shiny blue Cadillac.

When we got to the mall we went to the teen trendy stores and Momma let me pick out my clothes, with her approval of course. I picked out some cute little dresses, several pairs of pants, a few tops and for the first time, real lady bras. I was one of those girls who went from wearing training bras to a "C" cup over the summer. No longer did I look like the boys. I also began my *"woman days,"* as Momma called it. My body went through a metamorphosis that summer.

The night before the first day of school Momma pressed and curled my hair and I picked out my *"first day of school"* outfit. However, I was pretty self-conscience about my new body. It was as if I was a totally different person. Momma tried to comfort my concerns by telling me I had just blossomed into a young lady. She said it was a normal process all girls went through, but I was not comfortable with my newly "blossomed" body.

On the first day of school I spent what seemed like hours in the bathroom making sure everything was perfect. Things were much better at home since daddy had gotten a new job that required him to be out of town most of the time – that was a tremendous blessing. I loved him and had an incredible desire to be loved by him, but at the same time hated him with a perfect hatred.

When I was dressed I went into the kitchen for Momma's approval. "Oh, Angel, you look so pretty – your hair…those eyes…just beautiful. Not to mention how smart you are. You're going to have a great school year, I just know it."

"I sure hope you're right Momma."

On my way to school I thought maybe now the popular girls would like me. I had on nice clothes, my hair had been freed from the ponytail and we were all finally in the eighth grade. I thought maybe no one would recognize my blossoming. "Wow Angel, you look all grown up," Alex said when he walked in the room.

I hugged him, knowing he meant it as a compliment, but it didn't help my confidence at all. "Thank you Alex, you're looking very cute…I mean handsome yourself. Your shirt is sharp – I love that shade of blue. It brings out that nice brown skin tone of yours."

Nervously, I walked into Mrs. Stewart's 8th grade class; the first thing I noticed was that I had done a whole lot more "blossoming" than the other girls. This year my assigned seat was right behind my old friend Zachary. "Hey Zach," I said taking my seat.

"Heyyy...hey, Angel," he said as he turned around.

His mouth was hanging open and his eyes wide. "What's wrong with you Zach?"

"You look...you look so pretty. Can I touch your hair?"

"What?! No, you can't touch my hair, what's wrong with you, boy?"

That's the way all the boys responded that day. I didn't understand. Last year, they didn't act like that. These were the same boys I used to climb trees and play baseball with. The same boys I beat racing. What was this? Why were they acting like that?

The girls seemed to dislike me now more than ever. They said things like: "You think you're cute!" and "Who do you think you are?" I was so confused. These were not the responses I expected. I sat puzzled trying to figure it out when Rodney Walker, a new transfer student walked into the class room.

Rodney was so cute – big dark brown eyes, beautiful mocha skin, an afro the size of the moon and a smile that lit up the room like a 100 watt bulb. Every girl in the 8th grade wanted to be his girlfriend. They flocked around him like he was a movie star. I wouldn't dare to even dream he would ever be interested in me.

Of course, Rosie staked her claim. She quickly made her way over to him during lunch. I couldn't hear their conversation, but when she returned to the table she boldly announced, "Rodney is my boyfriend!" That settled it – no one dared cross Rosie.

One day during our lunch period, Rodney, in all his glory walked in and asked if he could sit with me. He was wearing a paisley long sleeve shirt with a large collar and dark blue bell bottom jeans. He smelled so good I couldn't speak. I just sat there. *'Say something idiot!'*

"Hey…can I sit with you?" He asked again.

"Uh, yeah…sure."

"What's your name?" He asked.

'What's my name?' "Um, uh Angel," I answered softly.

Rodney was such a gentleman and his eyes were so kind. We talked the entire lunch period. He told me his Daddy's job transferred him frequently, so their family moved a lot. He had a sister, but she was much older. I told him about Momma and Alex, but nothing about daddy. "I like talking with you Angel. May I have your phone number?" He asked politely.

 "Isn't Rosie your girlfriend?"

"No! Who told you that?"

"Rosie told everyone. You didn't ask her to be your girlfriend?"

"Nope, I didn't," he said firmly.

After that, I gladly gave him my phone number. I felt I was dreaming. Here I was, plain old stupid Angel, and Rodney, the coolest dude in the whole school, was sitting with me and wanted my phone number. This was by far the best day at school I had ever had! Momma was right!

I still didn't have any female friends and girls seeing me sitting next to Rodney, *"Rosie's boyfriend,"* made it worse. It wasn't long before word got back to Rosie and she confronted me. "Why were you talking to Rodney? You know he's my boyfriend."

"Rodney asked me for my phone number. If you have a problem with that you need to discuss it with him."

It's amazing what a little self-confidence will do for you. I just knew she was going to knock me out, but instead, to my surprise, she and her entourage just rolled their eyes, turned and walked away. Amazed, I turned around to find Rodney standing behind me. No wonder they walked away. "Yep, this is going to be a good school year after all."

CHAPTER 6

An orphanage opened in our neighborhood and the children who lived there were zoned to our school. We went to an all-black school until the kids from the orphanage began attending. Our school quickly became a blended community.

A girl name Terri Marshall came to our class and sat across from me. She had freckles and strawberry blond hair. Terri was my first female friend. She told me how their house burned down and her mother couldn't afford take care of her anymore. Terri was sure that one day, when her Momma got on her feet, she would come and get her and they would be a family again. I couldn't begin to imagine not living with my Momma.

The other kids would make fun of the kids from the orphanage, but Terri's story touched my heart. She sat at the lunch table with me and Rodney every day. After a few months she was sent to a foster home and I never heard from her again. As I grew older, I often wondered through the years what happened to her and if her mother ever came back to get her – I prayed she had.

It wasn't long before we were graduating from the 8th grade. We were on our way to high school. Now we would be little fish in a big ocean – I was excited. Unfortunately, Rodney's family moved after our graduation. Daddy didn't pay the bill, so our phone was turned off most of the summer and Rodney and I lost contact.

I really missed them. We had such fun together. I remember one day we were allowed to leave the school campus for lunch and the three of us walked to the ice cream store. We put our lunch money together and bought a banana split with extra cherries and whipped cream. We asked for three spoons and dug in. It was the best of times.

Terri loved to tell goofy jokes, but we laughed anyway. Rodney was our protector and treated us like princesses. I had finally found true friends. Friends as dear to me as my tree and it broke my heart to lose them. I will always cherish the memories of our 8th grade year together.

CHAPTER 7

The morning was crisp, the air had a slight chill to it and the trees in the park were ablaze with beautiful autumn colors of yellow, orange and red. It was September 15th, my first day of high school. I was extremely excited, but for all the wrong reasons.

Over the summer, I had mastered using my body and looks to get the attention I craved. My newly blossomed body wasn't so bad after all. Boys loved it and I loved the attention I was receiving. It was like being addicted to drugs, always in pursuit of the next high or in my case, the next boy who told me all the things I longed to hear.

While the kids in the neighborhood had backpacks filled with binders, notebooks, rulers and pencils, all I had was my phone book and a pen. No notebooks, no back pack and no paper. On the first day of school, I had gotten at least twenty phone numbers. I had done very well on the high school entrance placement test, so they put me in a first period advisory class with the smart kids, although I never felt smart. I didn't even try to keep up with my school work. My focus was totally on the boys and all the attention I could get from them. I had longed to be special to somebody for so long that anybody would do.

Since daddy needed the phone for his job when he was in town, he made sure the bill was always paid. It had been off for so long they gave us a new phone number. Now, I knew I would never hear from Rodney again. As soon as Momma went to bed the phone was attached to my ear for most of the night.

One particular night while talking to one of my many suitors, he asked if I was a virgin. Now of course I had no idea what virgin was, so I asked him to hold. "Hey, Momma, am I a virgin?!"

Now, I understand not knowing what virgin was at my age is unheard of in this generation, but for a church girl under the watchful eyes of her mother, it wasn't strange at all. "Who are you talking to young lady?"

Momma promptly came into the room, snatched the phone and hung it up and offered no explanation as to what a virgin was or whether or not I was one. The next day at school, I looked up the word, virgin. Yes, I was a virgin, but not for long.

My sophomore year began with me still looking for love in all the wrong places. That's the year I met a very popular senior named Stanley. He was very nice and always told me how beautiful I was.

Starving for affection, affirmation, and attention I didn't care who it came from. Stanley told me he loved me and wanted to be, "my first." He master minded a plan for us to meet and I willingly agreed. After all, he loved me and if you love someone you have to show them. Uncle Donny taught me that.

I must admit, deep down inside I knew it was wrong. Usually, when you have to keep things secret and lie to do it, it's wrong. I would lie and tell Momma I was going to the mall, then ride my bike to Stanley's house. He instructed me to knock three times on basement door and he would let me in. Of course, I followed his instructions to the letter and when he opened the door, there he stood in an unbuttoned black shirt showing his bare chest in his black denim jeans. Soft music played in the background and several candles sat on the table.

The next day he called and we talked about our intimate time together in great detail. He asked question after question. Shortly after our call, his mother called me.

You see, the telephone company had just come out with an amazing new feature called, "three-way-calling." You could have three people on the call at the same time. If the person you called also had that feature, you could have four people on the call.

Stanley's mother asked me if I knew that several of his friends were on the call listening to our whole conversation. She said they actually all placed bets to see who would be my first. "Those boys don't love you at all; they just want to get into your pants. Now, you're a girl with a bad reputation," she said with a motherly tone. Then she politely asked that I never come to or call her house again.

Tears streamed down my face like rain on a window.

I couldn't believe I was crying, but I was so hurt and confused. "He told me he loved me."

When you love someone you keep their secrets. I loved Momma, so I kept her secret about daddy beating us. I loved Uncle Donny, so I kept his secret about how he loved me. How could Stanley do that to me?! Could it be he was lying? Could it be that Uncle Donny lied? Even though their love was painful emotionally, it wasn't like the kind of pain Momma endured from daddy.

Love and sex became very convoluted, but yet I still longed for both. I thought if you love someone, you give them sex. They never talked about sex in church and I dare not ask Momma. They did talk about how God, our Heavenly Father, loved us, but given my experience with love and fathers, I never made the connection. God wasn't tangible to me.

In my senior year, I met a much older guy named Ivan. He had already graduated from high school, had a job and his own car. He told me he was nineteen, but he was really twenty-two. When I was with him I felt like a grown-up.

Ivan would take off work and I would cut class and go to his apartment. We started off just kissing, but it wasn't long before I understood that older men wanted to do more than just kiss. But after my last experience, I was a little hesitant to show my love for him.

It wasn't just about keeping a secret anymore. I absolutely knew what I was doing was wrong. Before I knew it, I had become quite a good liar. I was drawn not so much to Ivan, but the addiction and the thrill of the hunt in the pursuit of finding love. Whatever love was, this was the only way I knew to get it…or what I thought was *it*.

One day while at his apartment Ivan said I was too uptight and needed to relax. He walked over to his dresser, opened the drawer and pulled out what first appeared to be cigarettes. He explained to me that they were joints and if I smoked them with him I would feel free.

There were kids at school who talked about smoking weed and how good it made them feel, but I had never seen one before. Everything in me wanted to feel free. I wanted to feel good about me, about my life, about something – anything.

Ivan showed me how to inhale and it didn't take long for me to feel free. That day I showed him how much I loved him without any inhibitions. The next day he took me to get birth control pills, and then all limitations vanished.

The conviction I'd felt became dull. So much so, that I could hardly feel anything at all. Now that I was free, I wanted to love him every day. Every chance I got I was sneaking off with Ivan to his apartment to get high to show him love.

That summer I turned seventeen and was quite comfortable in my new freedom. Most seventeen year olds were usually not very responsible and it wasn't long before I began forgetting to take my birth control pills. After missing one period, then two, I knew I was pregnant. So I caught the bus to Ivan's apartment and waited for him to come home.

For three hours I occupied my time with thoughts of how to tell him. Sitting in the shade under a tree, I rehearsed the script in my head over and over, when finally I heard the squeal of his brakes. Immediately after, his 1970 red Regal pulled into the gate and he park in his assigned spot.

As soon as he got out of his car I walked toward him, and then stopped in my tracks when he walked to the passenger's side of his car and opened the door. I was just about to call to him when out stepped a woman. She was very pretty and looked about his age. He pulled her into arms and kissed her passionately.

Tears instantly filled my eyes. What should I do? I was so very angry, but I dare not say anything. I watched, heartbroken as he escorted her into his apartment and closed the door behind them. Slowly I walked to the bus stop wondering what I was going to do.

When I got home Alex greeted me at the door and instantly he could tell I had been crying. "What's wrong Angel?"

"Nothing, I just had something in my eye."

Alex reluctantly accepted my excuse and told me Momma wanted to see me. Before she saw me I ran to the bathroom to try to pull myself together. When I looked in the mirror it hit me. My breasts were larger and my pants were tighter. I went into her room and she asked me point blank, "Are you having sex?"

"No Momma, of course not," I lied.

"What am I going to do with you Angel? You know

better! The school called. They say you have been cutting class. Angel, what are you thinking! How are you planning on graduating if you're cutting classes? Where have you been going?" She snapped.

Of course I denied all charges. "Momma, I…"

Before I could tell another lie, she cut me off. "You're not going anywhere other than school for a whole month, do you hear me! Just go to your room!!! I don't know what to do with you anymore! What happened to my sweet Angel?"

As I walked to my room, I wondered what happened to her sweet Angel too. There was no way I could stay away from Ivan for a whole month. I needed him. I needed to get high. I needed to confront him about that woman.

The next night, when Momma went to sleep, I called and I asked him to come pick me up. I climbed out my bedroom window and met him on the corner and we drove to his apartment. "Ivan, do you love me?" I randomly asked.

"Of course I do."

"Then who was that woman I saw you with yesterday?"

"What?!"

"I came to your apartment and saw you kissing her."

"You been spying on me little girl?"

His tone was surprising; he had never talked to me like that before. "No, I just came over to tell you something…"

"If you ever talk to me like that again I'll break your neck!" he snapped.

"Ivan, I didn't mean to make you mad. I just saw you with her and…you said you loved me."

"I do love you, but I'm a man, baby and I have needs. Needs a little girl like you, can't fill. You understand don't you, baby?"

"Yeah, I guess so."

"Come here Baby, I've got something for you."

"You do?" My eyes brightened.

"Yeah, take this," he said handing me two pills.

"What is it?"

"Baby, it's even better than weed. It will make you feel so good that you'll love me like a real woman, not a little girl."

I wanted to love him like he wanted me to, so I took the pills and could almost immediately feel myself losing control. I didn't have a care in the world. Whatever it was must have been strong, because I passed out and when I came to it was five o'clock Sunday morning. "Ivan!!! Get up; you've got to take me home, now!!!"

My head was spinning and my heart was racing. He took his time getting up, threw on some pants and drove me home. As I climbed back into my bedroom window, I wasn't feeling very well. It wasn't more than twenty minutes after I had undressed, put my night gown on, and gotten in bed that Momma came into my room. "Good morning Angel, it's time to get up and get ready for church."

"I don't feel good, Momma."

"What's wrong Honey?" She asked sitting on the edge of my bed feeling my forehead for any sign of fever.

"It's just my period – really bad cramps," I lied. "I've been up most of the night."

"Oh, I'm sorry you're not feeling well baby. I guess you can stay home today, but you're going to miss the church dinner and the concert. We won't be back until tonight. I'll get you some aspirin, you should feel better soon. I'll call to check on you."

"Okay Momma, but I'm so tired, I'll probably be sleep, so don't worry if I don't answer."

As soon as I laid my head on my pillow I fell asleep, but sharp stomach cramps woke me. I made my way to the bathroom where I felt like I passed something large. I was so afraid. What were those pills Ivan gave me?

I called Ivan, no answer. So I called the emergency room at Bethany General Hospital and explained what was happening. The nurse told me to get to the hospital right away, but I was in so much pain I could barely walk.

When I called him again, he finally answered and I told him I was sick. Something was very wrong. When I asked him what were the pills he had given me he hung up. Fifteen minutes later he was rushing me to the emergency room. When we got there he made me use a fake name and told the registration nurse I was his wife. I thought it had a nice sound to it – Ivan's wife.

They asked for my ID, but Ivan told them that in his

rush to get me to the hospital we forgot to grab my purse and his wallet. He lied so convincingly that even I thought he really cared about me. He said he would go back home get it and bring it back after I was seen because he didn't want to leave my side. The nurse bought his story and I was immediately sent to the back to be seen by the doctor. By that time I had started hemorrhaging. Deep down I knew Ivan really stayed to make sure I didn't tell anyone he had given me drugs.

After the procedure was over and I had rested, the nurse told me I could put on my clothes and the doctor would be in to speak with us. Ivan and I sat in silence for what seemed like an eternity before the doctor finally knocked. "Come in," I said in a weak voice.

The doctor explained to me and my *"husband,"* that I was pregnant, but had a miscarriage. He had to perform a Dilation and Curettage, normally referred to as a (D&C), but I would be fine. He asked me if I had taken any drugs. Ivan chimed in defensively, "What are you trying to say doctor? My wife doesn't do drugs!!!"

Ivan grabbed me by the hand and stormed out of the room, down the hall and out the hospital doors. All the way home he cursed and called me stupid for forgetting to take my birth control pills. He told me he regretted getting involved with a little girl.

I apologized repeatedly and promised it would never happen again. We pulled in front of my house and I knew Momma and Alex would be home from church shortly. I begged him to forgive me, but he looked at me with a strangely familiar, terrifying look in his eyes, balled up his fist and punched me in my mouth.

My lip was instantly swollen. With blood running down my chin, I cried. "I'm sorry Ivan, it will never happen again!"

"See look what you made me do you stupid fool!!! Just get out of my car!"

I begged and pleaded with him to call me, then got out of his car. He sped off and I hurried into the house so the neighbors wouldn't see me. I tried to clean up as best I could and think up a lie to explain my swollen, busted lip before Momma and Alex arrived home, when I heard what I thought was Sister Green dropping Momma and Alex off. She was our regular ride to and from church every Sunday since Sister Johnson moved. But I was wrong; it was daddy arriving home from one of his frequent business trips.

He would actually pay to park the car at the airport while he was out of town rather than allow Momma use the car. I was sure he wouldn't even look at me to notice my swollen lip. I went into my room and closed the door as he gathered his things from the car. "Donna," he called.

"Hey daddy, Momma and Alex are at church. I stayed home 'cause I had cramps," I answered from my closed bedroom door. If by some great miracle he wanted to actually see me, I knew mentioning cramps would keep him from coming into my room. He didn't respond, but I wasn't surprised.

I cried myself to sleep hoping Ivan would call me and was startled by a knock on my bedroom door. "Momma brought you and daddy some dinner from church – you can come and eat."

"Alex, please tell Momma that I'm still not feeling well and I'm not hungry."

It wasn't long before Momma came into my room to check on me. I quickly pulled the covers up passed my mouth. "What's wrong Angel? You still feeling bad Sweetheart?"

When I heard the genuine concern in her voice, I knew she was not just worried about my cramps, but how I had changed and how she had caught me in several lies. "I'm okay Momma, it's just cramps. I just want to rest, so please don't worry."

Several minutes passed by before either of us spoke. "Angel, I'm praying for you. There's such greatness in you and I love you so much. Is there anything you want to talk about or anything I can do for you?"

I pretended to be asleep, but everything in me wanted to tell it all and let her know I loved her too. But the wall I had built around my heart was much too tall, wide and deep for the words to get pass.

As she kissed me on my forehead and gently closed the door, I cried. Where are all these tears coming from? I endured bad daddy for years and didn't shed a tear. Now, I couldn't seem to get my emotions in check. I guess I'm not as hard as I thought.

CHAPTER 8

The morning after, the sun pressed its way through the blinds that hung over my bedroom window. I awakened as sad and depressed as when I fell asleep. Before Momma got up, I slipped into the bathroom to shower. As I stepped into the shower, I got a glimpse of my lip in the mirror. The water mixed with my tears as I sank to the floor, tired and defeated. How I wished I could run across the street to the shelter and protection of my tree and hide there forever.

I promised myself I wouldn't call Ivan, he would have to call me and apologize. My lip was a constant, painful reminder of the previous day's drama. Looking at the clock on my nightstand, I tried to calculate when Ivan would be awake and if he would call before I left for school. With everything in me, I hoped the phone would ring.

My heart ached with every passing minute as I waited as long as I could before I had to leave to catch the bus to school. I began to rationalize why he hadn't called.

After all, it was my fault that I got pregnant. It was my fault that I forgot to take my pills. If I really think about it, I owed him an apology.

Sympathetically, I picked up the phone and dialed his number as fast as my fingers could dial...no answer. I wanted to leave him a message that sounded mature, so he would understand I wasn't a little girl, but a woman. All I needed was another chance to prove it to him.

Momma was stirring in the kitchen. The smell of fresh brewed coffee engulfed me as it seeped under my door. I knew she was making a big breakfast because daddy was home. My hopes were she would be too distracted cooking for him, to notice my lip.

'My battle scars actually looked much better,' I told myself. *'What was I going to tell Momma?'*

The door to the coat closet in our living room would stick, so you had to give it a good yank to open it. That's my story: *"I was trying to open the closet door and pulled it so hard it hit me in the mouth."* I thought it was pretty creative.

Either she bought my story or was too busy to deal with me. Momma struggled with depression and I certainly understood why. Food was her comfort and it didn't help that she was a great cook. I remember hearing her in the kitchen sometimes late at night opening the glass cake cover for yet another slice of delicious pound cake, or smelled the re-warmed leftovers that would have been our lunch the next day.

As I grew older so did her depression. She managed to perform her day to day duties, but did little else. Momma had absolutely no outdoor activities. I watched my daddy break her spirit. He literally drained her of her youth and vitality. With all she was going through, there I was adding to her pain. The pain I endured seemed to rule everything in my life. Hurting people are selfish like that.

———⊷———

An entire week passed without a return phone call from Ivan. Even after the multiple messages I'd left him. Finally, I decided to throw caution to the wind and caught the bus to his apartment. Once again, I lied to Momma and told her I was trying out for the track team, so I would be home late. I regretted lying even more so when she told me how happy she was about me trying out for the team.

When I arrived to his apartment I sat on the steps of the building adjacent to his and waited. Once again, I rehearsed what I would say. Over and over I prepared myself for the different scenarios of what his response might be. It played in my head like a motion picture. *'Just a few more minutes, he'll be home and I'll make everything right.'* I told myself as it began to get dark. Thirty minutes passed, still no Ivan. Slowly I walked to the bus stop hoping to see him along the way, but I didn't.

What was I going to do now? I thought about Stanley telling me he loved me too, but broke my heart. But I thought Ivan was different. How terribly wrong I had been. I never heard from or saw him again. I believe God answered Momma's prayers by removing Ivan from my life.

With him gone, my focus was back on my studies. I had a lot of work to do in order to catch up, but God gave me favor with my teachers and they allowed me to make up the work. They even gave me extra credit assignments and projects. It wasn't long before my grades were good and I was back on track to graduating. As crazy as it sounds, I missed Ivan and getting high.

One day Momma asked me what I wanted to be and the answer that came to my heart first was: loved. *"I want to be loved."* Of course, that wasn't my answer to her. "Oh, Momma, I don't know, maybe a teacher or a social worker."

"I'm glad you have dreams and goals. Angel, please, don't ever lose them."

Well into my senior year, I met Carmen and we quickly became friends. She was from New York, was tall with curly hair and spoke with a distinct accent. Her daddy was a radio personality and her mother was a stay-at-home-mom too. I introduced her to Momma, and they immediately connected.

Carmen and I did everything together. Homecoming was just around the corner and our football team was playing against their old rivals, The Kings. It was a great game, we won 28 to 21. After the game all the kids hung out at the local fast food restaurant. Carmen and I decided we would grab something to eat and hang out as well.

It seemed like everyone from the game was there. It was packed and the sound of chatter and laughter filled the place. We were laughing and talking when someone called my name. I turned around and to my surprise and delight it was Rodney, my 8th grade crush.

I couldn't believe he was actually standing in front of me. He must have had a growth spurt, because he was every bit of 6'5". There he stood wearing jeans and a University of Missouri jacket. Those same beautiful big brown eyes and amazing smile made my heart flutter. I jumped up and we hugged each other for what seemed like ten minutes. "Rodney, how are you?!"

"Much better, now that I've seen you!" he said charmingly.

"Hey, this is my best friend Carmen."

"Nice to meet you Carmen," he extended his hand.

"Nice to meet you too," she smiled.

"If you two will excuse me for just a minute, I see a friend I want to say hello to." Giving me a quick wink, she made her way out of the booth.

"Sure," Rodney said stepping to the side.

"So, catch me up. What's been going on in Angel's world?"

"Well, not a lot. You know – just school, homework, church and chores."

"Same here – how's your little brother, Alex doing? He's got to be a big guy now."

"Yes, he is – tall with big feet. He's a great kid. I see you are wearing a Missouri U jacket. Weren't we in the same grade?"

"Yes we were, but I went to summer school and took

a few college courses while I was in high school, so I graduated a year earlier."

"Wow, that's great. What about your family, Rodney? You guys moved a lot, huh?"

"Yeah, my dad's job moved him around a lot. He was building his career, so we went wherever they sent him. I tried calling you, but the number was disconnected."

"Umm, yeah, my dad had the number changed – prank callers," I lied.

"I understand. May I ask you for your new number?"

"Sure," I tried to keep my composure.

Rodney handed me a pen and grabbed a napkin off the table. I jotted my number down and handed him his pen. "I'll call you," he said excitedly.

"Looking forward to it!"

Carmen made her way back to the table with a big grin on her face. "Take care of our friend Carmen."

"Will do" she said as we watched him walk away. "Girl, I've got two questions. Who was that and does he have a brother?"

We both laughed as I shared my story of how I met Rodney and how much of a gentleman he was. "I have never met anyone like him."

"He sounds like an amazing guy."

"Yeah, he was back then, now he's a young man in college. They all change – you know what I mean. He probably has a harem now that he's in college."

"That's true for some men, but not all men," Carmen disputed.

"Well, it's true for all the ones I've known." We finish chit-chatting, cleaned our table and headed to the bus stop.

The bus was thirty minutes late when it finally arrived, the driver said he was late due to a very bad car accident. "One car had actually flipped over," he said. I prayed everyone would be okay.

"See you later Carmen." I said as I got off at my stop. As I turned the corner, I saw the flashing lights of an ambulance and police cars. My heart pounded as I started with a jog and then to a full sprint down the long block. Was it our house or Mr. and Mrs. Lucas's house? My heart sank when I realized it was our house. What happened? What had bad daddy done? Was Sister Johnson right, had he finally killed Momma?

I ran into the house and Alex was crying. "What's wrong, what's happened?!" I ask frantically.

"It's Momma. Daddy was yelling at her and she got dizzy and fell."

I looked at daddy; he just turned his head and looked away. "Where is she, where's Momma?!"

Alex pointed to their bedroom. I pushed my way through the police into their room. There was Momma, on the floor unconscious. I fell to the floor next to her and called her, but a paramedic pulled me away. "We're trying to help your mom sweetheart."

"Why don't you go take care of your brother?"

I didn't move. The police made way for the stretcher

as it was pushed down the hallway. In just a few minutes Momma was on her way into the ambulance. "Daddy, we gotta go the hospital!!!" I said frantically. He just looked at me, then at Alex, went into their room and closed the door.

"Let me through, I'm their next door neighbor!" I heard Mr. Locus explain.

I grabbed Alex's hand and ran to him. "Mr. Locus, please, something's wrong with Momma. Can you take us to the hospital?"

"Yes of course, sure. Let me find out where they're taking her."

Within a few minutes we were on our way. "What happened? Was it your dad?"

"No," Alex said still wiping his tears. "He was yelling at her then she got dizzy and fell. Angel, she hit her head on the floor so hard. She's gonna be okay, right?"

I held Alex close and tried to be brave, but I was so very afraid. "God, please, let her be okay."

We arrived at City General Hospital and parked in the spaces reserved for the Emergency Room. Mr. Lucas told us to sit down while he went to check on Momma. A few minutes later, he came back and told us the doctors were doing all they could and he believed she would be fine.

It seemed like an eternity before the doctor finally called for us. He told us that Momma had an aneurism and wasn't responsive. He asked Mr. Lucas was he related to Momma. "No Sir, I'm the next door neighbor, I just brought the kids here."

The doctor then turned his attention to me, "Sweetheart, where is your father?"

"I don't have a father."

Alex looked at me puzzled, "Yes we do Angel, daddy's at home." Then he gave the doctor our phone number.

"When can we see her? That's all I wanna know," I demanded.

"In just a little while, sweetheart."

"Mr. Lucas, may I speak with you in the office please?"

"Of course."

"Kids, I'm going to speak with the doctor, but I'll be right back. Angel, take care of Alex."

About thirty minutes later, daddy arrived. Mr. Lucas stopped him at the door and filled him in on what the doctor said. Alex had fallen asleep, so I moved a few seats closer to hear what they were talking about. "The doctor said it doesn't look good John. They're doing all they can, but it doesn't look good."

Mr. Lucas's eyes filled with tears. He turned his head so I couldn't see him. I felt so lost and alone. "Not Momma, she's good and kind," I prayed.

Just then the doctor called daddy's name. He and Mr. Lucas walked over to the doctor as I read his lips. "We tried everything we could – she's gone."

I couldn't breathe, I couldn't speak. What happened? What just happened? I couldn't think. I had to see her.

Slowly, I walked up to the doctor. "Where is she? I want to see my Mother!"

"Sweetheart…"

"I'm not your sweetheart!!! I want to see my mother, now!!!"

The doors opened as someone was coming out of the trauma unit and I ran in. Momma was just lying there. Machines all around her and tubes still connected to her lifeless body. People were everywhere. I pushed them all out of the way and climbed into the bed. I cried and pleaded with her not to go. "Momma, please don't go. Please, come back to us!!!"

It was too late, she was already gone. I ached so deeply for her to say or do something. I couldn't speak. I could only groan, that's what I did for the rest of the night.

CHAPTER 9

The phone rang I answered hoping it was Rodney. I so needed someone to talk to and was looking forward to speaking with him. As bad as I wanted to talk to Rodney, it wasn't his voice on the other end. I wasn't surprised when he didn't call – hurt, but not surprised.

It was Uncle Keith calling to check up on us. Daddy must have called and given him the tragic news, because I could tell he had been crying. "It's so good to hear your voice Angel. How…how are you guys doing?"

For a few seconds, I couldn't speak. "It's so crazy Uncle Keith. I don't understand – why Momma? Why now?"

"Angel, I'm on the next flight home. I'll be there first thing tomorrow morning."

"Okay Uncle Keith, we'll be so glad to see you. Hurry, please."

"I will baby, I will."

"Love you Uncle Keith."

"Love you too, and give my love to Alex and your dad."

"Okay, see you tomorrow. Bye."

Uncle Keith had no idea what kind of man daddy really was and I couldn't wait to tell him everything. He'll take Alex from daddy and send me off to college. No need to rehearse this time, I knew exactly what I would say. Morning couldn't come soon enough.

The doorbell rang at 7:25am and I knew it was Uncle Keith. I flung open my bedroom door and was startled by daddy standing there. "Listen to me, and listen good, don't you open your mouth about anything that went on in my house do you hear me?! It was me and your Momma's business," he growled.

The doorbell rang again. "If you say anything to him, I'll take Alex, we'll go away and you'll never see him again. I swear I'll do it. Now, put a smile on that pitiful face of yours and go answer the door." Everything in me knew he meant what he said. I had just lost Momma, I couldn't lose Alex too. As I walked to the door I felt defeated, but it would still be so good to see Uncle Keith. When I opened the door I melted in his arms as we both cried.

Two days later, black funeral limos lined up in front of our house in a gruesome procession. Carmen and I sat in my room; neither of us said a word. I knew she wanted to comfort me, but there simply were no words anyone could say to ease the pain of losing Momma.

Daddy was helping Alex with his tie, while Uncle

Keith was getting dressed. Sister Johnson arrived shortly after the limos. Her voice was music to my ears. I bolted from my room and ran into her arms. She held me tight and I never wanted her to let go. If she let go, I would simply fall to pieces. "What are me and Alex gonna do?!"

"God's got you child."

"God didn't have Momma," I pulled away from her.

"You stop that foolish talk Angel! Where do you think she is now? She's in the arms of Jesus and she's at peace. Now, where's that daddy of yours?"

"In Alex's room."

Sister Johnson didn't knock; she just opened the door and went in. I wanted to hear what she was saying, but I just didn't have the strength to listen. When Alex knocked on my door, I knew she had sent him into my room so she could speak freely with daddy.

A few minutes later, daddy walked out of the room. I couldn't believe he was crying. Anger instantly rose within me. *'Oh, now you wanna cry! Don't you dare shed a tear. You made her life miserable. You did this! It's your fault, I hate you!!!'* I thought.

I was so angry. I was angry with daddy. I was angry with myself, I was angry with doctors. I was angry with God. "Why did you take Momma? I don't understand. She loved You so much, God. I just don't understand."

Daddy, Alex, and Uncle Keith rode in the limo, while I rode with Sister Johnson. We rode quietly for a while, before she broke the silence with a sigh. "Angel, I know you're hurting something terrible, but your Mother is in a better place."

I was so sick of hearing that! "Well, I want her here. I want her here now, with me and Alex. Oh, my God! What about Alex? What's going to happen to him? What's going to happen to me?" I panicked.

"Well, Sweetheart, you're just about grown now. You'll be graduating in a few months."

"Oh no, graduation! Momma won't be here to see me graduate. It's so cruel!"

"Oh yes, your Momma will see you graduate! She will have the best seat in the house. She'll be watching you from Heaven."

The funeral was a blur. I only remember the singing and how kind and caring the people at the church were. They loved Momma so much. The choir sang her favorite song, *"Jesus, There's Something About That Name."*

There's something else I remember that was very strange. There was a woman, not quite as tall as daddy who wore a black dress and a big black hat with a veil that covered most of her face. I leaned over to Sister Johnson and asked her who the mysterious woman was in the black dress. She studied her for a while, and said, "I don't know sugar, never seen her before."

After the service, I was holding Alex's hand next to Sister Johnson and Uncle Keith as the church members gave their condolences, when I saw the lady in the black dress again. My first thought was that she was some woman daddy had been cheating on Momma with. She walked up to daddy and reached out to hug him, but he turned away. She grabbed his shoulders and turned him to face her. I couldn't hear what she was saying, but I knew I was wrong about her being daddy's mistress. I tried to get a glimpse of her face behind the veil and to my amazement she looked just like him.

I released Alex's hand and walked toward her. She saw me coming and hurried away. Immediately I went after her. I had to know who she was, but daddy grabbed my arm as I stormed past him. "Where you going, girl?"

"Who was that lady daddy? She looked just like you."

"She's nobody, now mind your business," he said walking out of the church. I watched to see if he was going to talk to her, but he got in one of the limo's and closed the door. Who was that strange woman and why was daddy so angry with her?

I watched the Pallbearers place Momma's casket into the hearse in preparation for the drive to the cemetery. At that moment, I was so angry with God. Momma loved Him. She served Him, but He didn't save her. He knew she was all I had in this world and allowed her to die. It just wasn't fair. It wasn't right. God needed to explain Himself to me!

Sister Johnson stayed for several days after the funeral then returned to North Carolina, but came by to see me and encourage me every day until she left. Uncle Keith was granted leave for two weeks to make sure we were alright. Alex and I talked with him for hours every day after school and on the weekends. He took us to the movies, the mall and out to dinner several times. He even invited Carmen to some of our outings.

There were so many times I wanted to tell him everything, but he spoke of how great his career was going and how he had met a special lady. I remembered Momma saying it wasn't fair to burden him with her problems, so I never told him anything.

The two weeks with Uncle Keith seemed to fly by. I heard him talking to daddy the day before he left. He really didn't know daddy very well. He joined the Air Force before he and Momma were married, so they really never had gotten a chance to get to know each other. When he called, daddy just exchanged the normal niceties and gave the phone to me, momma, or Alex. Uncle Keith asked daddy if there was anything he could do to help. Of course daddy declined.

We drove Uncle Keith to the airport and daddy didn't even help him with his bags. Alex and I hugged Uncle Keith tight; neither of us wanted him to leave. "Angel, I know you'll be going to college soon, so I'm going to send you money every month to help out. If you and Alex need anything, I mean anything, just let me know."

"Angel, I have something for you," he said reaching into his duffle bag, pulling out a poorly wrapped box.

No one spoke as we drove home. The silence was only broken by the rattling of paper as I opened the gift Uncle Keith gave me. To my surprise it was a picture of him and Momma when they were little, enclosed in a beautiful glass picture frame.

It must have been Easter Sunday, because they were both dressed in their Sunday's best. Momma had on a little yellow and white dress with an eyelet collar, white tights and white patent leather shoes. Her hair was in the cutest spiral curls with a yellow satin ribbon. Uncle Keith was wearing navy blue shorts with a navy and white seersucker jacket, long white socks and navy and white banister shoes and was holding a chocolate bunny.

Instantly, it became my most treasured possession. My eyes immediately filled with tears as I held it to my heart all the way home. I treasured not only the picture, but the thought as well.

CHAPTER 10

It had been four months since Momma went to be with the Lord. Daddy and I only spoke when it was absolutely necessary. Alex was getting along pretty well, but some nights I could hear him crying. When I would go into his room he would quickly wipe his face so I wouldn't know he'd been crying. Singing Momma's favorite songs seemed to soothe him and give him peace.

Uncle Keith kept his promise and called us faithfully every week. He also sent me $500 every month, which certainly came in handy. It meant I didn't have to ask daddy for anything.

The folks from church came to pick me and Alex up on Sunday mornings. Our Pastor preached about the love and the mercy of God and I would sit there wondering, where was His love for Momma. With each passing Sunday, my heart grew colder and the wall around my heart fortified. It wasn't long before I stopped going to church.

Watching the news at night, I would hear reports of

people committing all kinds of crimes, leaving a trail of victims, not to mention the hell daddy put us through. Why did God allow them to live? I just couldn't get her death to make sense.

I was done, but Alex continued going to church faithfully and was very active in the youth group. I knew he missed Momma, but he never seemed to be angry about her death. Even in his sadness, he walked in constant peace – I couldn't understand. He was growing into a pretty amazing young man.

Graduation was fast approaching, but it was so hard to focus in school and keep my grades up. I wasn't one of those naturally smart people. I really had to study and study hard to make good grades. So, Carmen and I would have study sessions and quiz each other. I knew Momma dreamed of the day I would graduate and I was determined not only to graduate, but to do it with honors.

During class one day my teacher told me the counselor needed to see me immediately. Instantly I dreaded what she would tell me. My heart raced as I made my way through the halls and down the two flights of stairs to the counselor's office. *Maybe, she would tell me I didn't have enough credits to graduate. Maybe, during my Ivan days, I cut too many classes. Maybe, I wouldn't graduate!* My thoughts were all over the place.

I knocked on the door to Mrs. Foster's office with a lump in my throat. "Come in," she said in a very stern voice.

I prepared myself for the inevitable as I slowly walked to the chair positioned across from her desk.

"Oh, come in Angel, come in. I guess you're wondering why I called you to my office," she said looking directly into my eyes.

"Yes, Ma'am. Is everything okay?"

"It's not only okay, it's great. Angel, I know you've had some issues, but I always knew you could do the work if you just applied yourself. So I took the liberty and used some of your essays to apply for some scholarships on your behalf. Since you're graduating with honors, you have received several scholarships!"

"I'm so very proud of you Angel. I know it's been really tough with your mom passing and all, but you did it! I know she would be so very proud of you."

I didn't know what to say. I did it…I really did it!!! I finally did something right. Everything in me knew Mrs. Foster was right, Momma was very proud of me. I believed God Himself gave her the good news. Excited about the wonderful news, I jumped up and gave Mrs. Foster a big hug and hurried out the door. Uncle Keith, Sister Johnson, Alex, and Carmen are going to be so excited when I tell them the wonderful news.

Just as I made it back to class the bell rung, so I quickly made my way to Carmen's locker and waited for her. When she came around the corner I ran and hugged her. "Carmen, I did it! I really did it!"

"You did what? What did you do?"

"I'm graduating with honors, just like Momma wanted!"

"That's the best news I've heard all month Angel,

I'm so happy for you! We gotta celebrate, how about the mall."

"Sounds great, let's meet at the food court. As soon as I get Alex's dinner ready, I'll hop on the bus and meet you there."

"Okay, see you in a little while Angel."

"Yep, see ya."

I got home and made spaghetti for Alex in record time. Before he could swallow his last bite of food we were heading out the door. "Hey, Angel, where are we going?"

"I'm going to the mall with Carmen to celebrate."

"To celebrate what?"

"Alex, I'm going to college!!! I even got a scholarship!!!"

"That's great Angel!" He congratulated me; however, I heard a little sadness in his voice.

"You're going over to Mr. Lucas's house; Carmen and the mall are waiting for me. I asked Mr. Lucas to watch you."

"Angel, I don't need a babysitter. You've gotta stop treating me like a baby!"

"I know Alex, but I just want to be on the safe side, please don't fuss."

"Okay, okay!" he said reluctantly.

Mr. Lucas was so very kind to us and was always willing to help. He and Mrs. Lucas were such good neighbors. I knew he knew what went on in our house the night Momma died; he asked me if daddy hurt Momma. I wondered why he never called the police. I guess he just tried to help in other ways.

After running two blocks, I anxiously waited for the bus when a car pulled up to the curb. I stepped back a bit, not recognizing the car and couldn't see the driver because of the glare from the sun. The driver's door flung open and I squinted to see the tall figure that stepped out. I couldn't believe my eyes – it was Rodney Walker. At first I was excited, but then my smile faded when I remembered he had promised to call me the last time I saw him.

"Angel! God certainly answers prayer! I am so glad to see you. How have you been?"

"I'm good," I said with a little attitude. "Last time I saw you, you said you were going to call me. Months later I'm still waiting for that call!"

"I know Angel, I'm so very sorry about that. I've replayed that day at the restaurant in my head many, many times. Angel, do you remember that day after the game?"

"Yeah…and?!"

"Well, when I pulled out of the parking lot that day, some guy that had too much to drink slammed right into me. I can't remember much after that. I woke up in the hospital three days later with broken ribs, a fractured leg and ankle and trauma to my brain. Of course, I have no idea what happened to the napkin with your number on it. But I've thought of you often, Angel. I wished I had asked where you lived. So I just prayed that God will bless me to see you again."

"Oh, my goodness, I'm so sorry Rodney! You know, I do remember my friend Carmen and I waited quite a while for the bus that day. The driver said there was a terrible accident. I had no idea you were involved. Please forgive me!"

"There's nothing to forgive Angel. God took great care of me. There was no permanent damage and now I'm a hundred percent. I'm pretty much a walking miracle."

"I would have never known you had been in a serious accident, you look great."

"What about you Angel, what's going on with you?"

"Well, my mom passed a few months ago," I tried to hold back the tears.

"Oh, wow Angel. I'm so sorry. What happened?"

"An aneurism – it was so sudden. I miss her so much. I can't believe God would allow her to die like that. She was such a wonderful woman. It just isn't fair."

"I can only imagine how you feel and how hard it must be. But even in tragedy God has plan. We may not understand, but He's still God."

"Yeah, well, God and I aren't on the greatest terms right now, so…"

"How is your Dad and Alex doing?" He interrupted.

"Alex is good, he's so grown up."

"I bet he is. What about your dad?"

"What about him?" The bitterness and hatred that coursed through those words must have shocked Rodney a bit. He had no idea about the hell that went on in our home – nobody did, except Sister Johnson and even she didn't know how he abused me.

"Okaaayyy...well, how are you Angel?"

"It's the hardest thing I've ever had to go through, and believe me; I've been through some things."

"Things like what?"

I ignored his question. "Oh, Rodney, I miss her so much it aches. But I just received scholarships to several colleges and I know how important it was to Momma that I get my degree."

"I know she's proud of you Angel, I am too. So what university will you be attending?"

"Lexington University, and I can't wait to get there, graduation will be here before you know it."

"That's a great school, good choice. So, where were you headed? Can I give you a lift?"

"I was just going to the mall to hang out with Carmen. We're celebrating my scholarships. You're welcome to join us."

"I really wish I could, but I have a meeting at my church. I work with the youth and we're planning for camp this summer. But please, let me take you to the mall."

"Sure Rodney, that would be great, thanks." We had great conversation on the way to the mall, but I was doing most of the talking. Rodney was so easy to talk to and was an excellent listener. Hoping to gain some insight, I asked him a million questions about college life and he patiently answered each one. I was amazed at the wisdom with which he spoke.

The scent of his cologne filled the car and I was captivated by his beautiful big brown eyes. He had the kind of eyes that made you want to gaze into the depths of them. There was so much peace and strength in them.

When we pulled up to the mall, I don't know why, but I was so nervous. Part of me didn't want the moment to end. "Angel, it's wonderful seeing you again. I've always enjoyed talking with you and you're even prettier than I remembered."

"Why thank you kind, Sir. That's very sweet of you," I blushed.

"You're very welcome, my Lady."

"It's good seeing you again too Rodney."

"Angel I want to make sure I have all of your information this time. I want to keep in touch." He asked for my number, address, the name of my high school, the date, time, and place of my graduation, and then chuckled as he asked for my social security number. "I'm going to call you Angel."

"I'm looking forward to it Rodney, be careful, no more accidents!"

"Trust me, one was more than enough. Bye."

I was grinning from ear to ear and couldn't wait to find Carmen and tell her about Rodney. We finally spotted each other in the Food Court. "Hey Girl – Angel, you did good. I know your Momma is smiling down from Heaven right now. So, have your decided on a school yet?"

"Yep, Lexington University. I also thought about how we talked about going to the same college and being roommates. I still want to do that. We have so little time to plan. We've gotta get bedding, towels, pillows, and…"

"Angel, I would love for us to be roomies and I know we've talked about it a million times, but the truth is, I'm not smart like you. I haven't even applied to any Universities. You have always been in classes with the smart kids and your grades are excellent. My GPA isn't that great."

"Smart? Who's smart? Carmen, I'm not smart. I was placed in those advanced classes in high school because of my reading test scores. You see, I had already read all of the short stories on the test. Our reading teacher assigned them to us and then we went over the answers in class. I don't know if it was just a coincidence or if she knew those exact short stories would be on the test. In any case, that's how I got placed in the advanced classes."

"Carmen, the grades I have now, I worked like crazy to earn for Momma. I messed up so much when she was alive and had so many regrets, I did it for her."

"It doesn't matter Angel, the fact is you did it. You're my best friend and that will not change no matter what. I'll talk to my Mom tonight. I don't even know if we can afford college."

"There are grants and loans available Carmen, it will work out, it just has to."

"Oh, with all this talk about school, I almost forgot. Guess who dropped me off at the mall?"

"Who?"

"Rodney!"

"Rodney – you mean, *the* Rodney?"

"Girl, yes!"

"Did you let him have it for not calling you?"

"I was going to give him an ear full until he told me he had a terrible car accident that same day you met him at the restaurant."

"Oh, my goodness! Was he hurt?"

"Yes, he didn't regain consciousness for three days. In all the drama, of course he had no idea what happened to the napkin with my number on it."

"That's certainly understandable. Is he okay now?"

"He said God took great care of him, he's totally healed."

"Was he still fine and gorgeous?"

"Absolutely, and he is doing very well in college."

"That's so cool. I'm still wondering if he has a brother, cousin, friend or somebody."

"I'll remember to ask when I talk to him," I laughed.

Carmen and I walked and talked until the mall closed, and all the way home on the bus. As I hurried to pick up Alex, I reflected again on the conversation with Rodney and the news of the scholarships. It was a little late, but I was going to call Uncle Keith and Sister Johnson anyway to tell them the great news. What a wonderful day it had been.

CHAPTER 11

Several days had passed and no call from Rodney. My imagination ran wild. I hope nothing has happened to him. Maybe he was just being a nice guy and I was just an old friend to him. But I really thought I felt something special when he hugged me. Maybe he met some gorgeous college chick and had forgotten all about me. What was I thinking; I should have asked him for his phone number.

Just then, bad daddy flung the door open. "Hey you little whore, some little thug called my house asking for you!" He was yelling as he walked toward me with that same look of hatred and disgust in his eyes. I immediately held up my hands to protect my face.

"No daddy, no! I'm sorry, I'm sorry. It was just my old friend from school, that's all. He's just a friend."

"I don't care who he is. I told him he had better not ever call this house again and I'm having the number changed. I can call the phone company and check all the calls coming in and going out Angel, so even when I'm out of town, I'll know. You think I don't know about you Angel. You fooled your Momma, but not me."

"What, what are you talking about? I don't know what you're talking about."

"You don't think I know you've been giving it up to every little punk you meet?" He walked towards me and touched my face. "Now Angel, your momma ain't here to protect you anymore. So since you're so use to giving it up, now you're gonna give it to me."

"Alex!!!" I screamed

"Shut the hell up!" He said as he grabbed a fist full of my hair. Then he put the other hand over my mouth. "Alex is a man just like me, he understands. He ain't here no way, and if you ever tell anybody anything, I just don't know what might happen to little Alex – you know, accidents happen."

"Your Momma's gone Angel, and I have needs. I've been watching you for a long time. You ain't a little girl anymore." He ripped open my blouse and slapped me. When I fell onto the bed I fought him as he climbed on top of me. He...he raped me. Daddy raped me."

When he finished he got up and wiped his mouth. "I knew you weren't no virgin!!! Clean your nasty self up and make me some dinner."

I laid there unable to feel. I couldn't think. I couldn't breathe. I never thought daddy would...who can I tell? What can I do? Where can I go? That's when the thoughts first entered my mind. *Just end it all. Who would miss you? Do it quickly. Just get some of those pills Ivan gave you, it won't hurt. Do it, do it now!!!'*

The moment I began to entertain the thought of suicide, Alex came to my mind. Now, I believed he was capable of hurting Alex. He's capable of anything. What did I do to make him…? What's wrong with me!!! Daddy made me "give it up," until the day I left for college. Each time I just laid there with hatred coursing through my veins.

Of course, I never got the opportunity to speak with Rodney, daddy made sure of that. I wished I had a way to get in touch with him. I felt like he was the only person on earth I could be completely honest with. I had so much pain stored in my heart, but felt I had no way to release it. I couldn't tell Carmen. She would tell her mother, who would quickly call the police and who knows what daddy would do.

I was still in a daze when Uncle Keith and Alex helped me move into my dorm room. That should have been one of the happiest days of my life. Instead I was completely depressed.

Sadly, Carmen wasn't accepted into Lexington, so I was on my own. I became distant and withdrawn. The bubbly personality I once had was gone. Uncle Keith and Carmen knew something was wrong and begged me to let them help. They just didn't understand. Nobody could help me. Even though I wasn't in his house anymore, daddy still controlled me with the threat of hurting Alex.

I had pictured the excitement of moving into and

decorating my dorm room many times before daddy did what he did. Now, it was just another thing I had to do, but I was still determined to make it beautiful. Even in my depressed state, my room was beautiful. I love color, so my twin sized comforter was rich jewel tone colors in a fun floral and paisley print. It had a matching pillow sham, with beaded matching throw pillows. To the left of my bed was a desk. It was small, but sufficient for studying and homework. There was a small closet and a bathroom I shared with three girls.

Cute little storage bins slid under my bed which housed my personal items, snacks, and school supplies. To my right, at the head of my bed was a night stand that held my most precious possession, the picture Uncle Keith had given me. I positioned it so every morning when I woke up it would be the first thing I'd see.

Iverem was my older Nigerian roommate. She told me that her name meant "blessings." She was six feet tall and had the most beautiful dark brown skin, perfectly white teeth, and spoke with a heavy accent. Her side of the room was decorated with elegant African fabrics of different textures and colors. I was really looking forward to getting to know her, but unfortunately, her boyfriend had his own apartment, so she rarely stayed in the dorm.

The campus at Lexington University in Jefferson City was beautiful and only three hours from Springfield. The sunlight danced through the tops of the mature trees that lined the walkways. The architectural details of each of the buildings were amazing. They stood tall and majestic and seemed to demand reverence. I read in one of the pamphlets that some rich guy donated money to have a prayer garden built somewhere on the campus. Of course, I didn't have much use for prayer, so no need to visit.

The first few days on campus I was in such emotional turmoil that my mind was plagued with all kinds of negative thoughts. All I wanted was not to feel or think. Thoughts of getting high quickly re-entered my mind. It was the only way I knew to get away from it all. So, as soon as I was all moved in, my search began.

I was on a college campus, so it didn't take long for me to find a dealer. As a matter of fact, I was amazed at how easy it was. I bought the weed, the papers, and rolled my joints with great anticipation. The campus provided many secluded areas surrounding the dorms. I found the perfect spot under a tree and smoked until I didn't care anymore.

What daddy did was the final nail in my coffin. I was a walking dead woman. Every day I went to my new tree and puffed all my cares away. My dealers name was Marlon. He had a small apartment right outside of campus. It was always dimly lit and cold. He burned incense to cover the smell of the weed and other unpleasant odors in the tiny space. It was the kinda place that gave you the creeps. The apartment actually matched his dark, shady character, but I didn't care as long as he had the drugs, it was all good.

School was going pretty well. I got a co-op job in the administrative office where I answered phones, filed, and performed other small tasks. If I wasn't studying or working, I was getting high. Being alone with my thoughts was just too painful, so I tried to stay busy.

From time to time Sister Johnson called to check on me and tell me that the Lord had me and would 'work all things together for my good.'

"My good – yeah, right!" She had no clue about the things I had suffered. However, it was always comforting to hear her voice. Carmen called often, but I would tell her I was busy or just not answer. I felt bad because she was such a good friend, but I didn't want her to know what kind of life I was living...what kind of person I'd become.

I didn't get to see Alex as often as I liked, because I never wanted to go to daddy's house, but I talked to him several times a week. He said he was doing well and had made the football team and was busy with practice. He often told me how much he missed me. I missed him too, but I knew Uncle Keith was keeping in touch with him.

Uncle Keith's request to be stationed closer to us was granted and now he was just a few hours away. He was able to visit Alex often and even attended some of his football games. It gave me a great measure of peace concerning Alex, but I was still a mess.

One Saturday evening Alex called me after one of his games. "Hey Angel, how are ya doing?"

"Hey little brother, I'm good. What'cha been up to?"

"I just got home from my game. We won 27 to 20, and yours truly scored the winning touchdown."

"That's so cool Alex. I'm so proud of you. Was Uncle Keith there?"

"Yep, and you know he took a ton of pictures. I'll send you some. Coach said the newspapers were there, so my picture may be in the paper too."

"Look at you, a celebrity and all. I'm glad Uncle Keith was there to celebrate with you. I'll bet there are a lot of pretty girls that would love to be the girlfriend of the school football champ. Do you have a girlfriend Alex?"

"Well, there is this girl at church I've got my eye on. Her name is Leslie."

"Leslie, that's a pretty name. I bet she's pretty too."

"Yep, she's really pretty and smart as well. She always knows the answers to Bible questions Sister Brock asks in our youth class at church."

"Oh, so you've got you a church girl. That's good Alex. She sounds very sweet."

"When you come home to visit, maybe you could meet her. By the way, when are you coming home, Angel?"

"Umm, I don't know Alex. College is hard work, with my classes, studying, and working, I'm not sure."

"It's cool, I understand."

"Be sure to tell Uncle Keith I said hello. I miss you both. Oh, and tell Leslie, I said hello too."

"Whatever…hope to see you soon, Sis."

"Love you little Brother and I'll talk to you soon."

"Love you too. Bye."

"Goodbye." I hung up the phone wishing things were different. I wished I could look forward to going home like normal kids.

Soon, the weed wasn't enough to dull the pain and I was constantly agitated. No wonder they call it *"the gateway drug."* I'm convinced that most people abuse drugs to escape some kind of pain or trauma. I was one of those people, so I went to visit Marlon.

"Hey Marlon, your weed is sweet, but uh, I need something a little bit sweeter, ya know what I mean."

"Oh, so you wanna hang with the big dogs now? You know I got just what you need, baby."

"I bet you do. What you got for your little Angel?"

"You got the bread?"

"Baby, you know I'm good for it."

"Naw Baby, I don't extend credit, but…you do have something I been wanting," he said looking me up and down, licking his nasty blackened lips.

In my desperation I responded, "You make me feel good and I'll make you feel good. Now, what you got for me?"

"How 'bout a little powder?"

"Powder?"

"Yeah girl, sugar, snow, candy…cocaine. It will take you on a high you'll never forget."

"Let's do it, Baby."

Marlon cut the cocaine with a razor and lined it up on his glass coffee table. He rolled up a hundred dollar bill and showed me how to snort it. The powder had a sweet taste to it and soon I didn't have a care in the world!!! When it was time to pay up, I kept my promise.

I had done it – I crossed the line. I was in a place I never thought I would be. But this is who I was; this is what I deserved, so it was inevitable. But, I couldn't keep the pretense up with Carmen. The last time we talked she said, "Angel, I don't know what's going on, but I know it's not good. If you won't talk to me or anybody else, please talk to God. I love you and I'll never stop praying for you."

Little did Carmen know or anyone else, that I no longer believed I was capable of being loved. And talk to God? He didn't want to hear from me. I was sure He wouldn't listen anyway. Where had he been when daddy was beating me and Momma? Where had he been when Uncle Donny forced me to keep his secret? Where was he when daddy was raping me? Where was he when Momma died? As far as I was concerned, God didn't care about me or my life. But I couldn't blame Him – I didn't even care about me.

It wasn't long before Marlon and I were a couple. A couple of what's, I'm not sure. Marlon was very paranoid. One day he called me, and I didn't answer. I was trying to cram for an exam and didn't have time to deal with him. Even though I was a drug addict, I was determined to finish school for Momma's sake. She was my only link to reality and sanity.

After class I went to his apartment. He opened the door, I walked in and before I could say a word he knocked me out. When I came to, he was standing over me with a bag of powder. "If you want to keep getting this good stuff, I am your priority."

"Baby, I had to study for an exam," I tried to explain.

"I don't care nothing about you studying. When I call, you better answer!" The language he used and the names he called me were awful. He balled his fist again and I braced myself for the next blow. But rather than hit me again, he spit on me, walked into the bathroom and closed the door.

I tried to sit up, but immediately felt the pain of his punch. My jaw was stiff and hurt so bad I thought it was broken. As usual I immediately began to think of a lie to explain what happened. *'It's an abscess, but I have an appointment with the dentist tomorrow. Yep, that would be my story this time.'*

As I struggled to my feet, my head was pounding and the blaring noise from the TV made it worse. That's until I heard a sweet familiar voice...

The Voice: "We are preparing to assist two hundred at risk, abused kids this year with food, clothing, counseling and a two week camping trip next summer."

The Reporter: "That's impressive. Is there a cost?"

The Voice: "God has blessed many of us to sow into the lives of these kids. Not only with our time, but our resources as well, so there's no cost to participate."

The Reporter: "Thank you for your time, and special thanks to you and your team for making a difference in these kid's lives"

The Voice: "You're very welcome, but I give all the glory to God."

The Reporter: "Is there a number people can call if they want more information about your program and the ministry?"

The Voice: "Sure, they can call 555-1255, we'll be glad to help."

The Reporter: "Thanks again Rodney, great job. This is Doug Roberts reporting, Channel 4 News."

It was Rodney, and he was doing well. I knew he would. I was just grateful I didn't get the chance to mess up his life like I had messed up mine. My moment of reflection was shattered when Marlon came out of the bathroom. "You want some of this?" he smirked, holding the stuff I had made my god.

"Yeah, please."

"Come do me then. You got to earn it."

How I hated those words with a perfect hatred. Sex had become nothing more than a commodity – simply something traded to get what I wanted. A beautiful body was the only thing I felt I had. Using it to barter was the only thing I was good at. But I had never once enjoyed it – ever. It was a necessary evil. There were times when I was so high I didn't even know or care what I was doing.

The beatings became more frequent, no matter how good I tried to be or how happy I tried to make him. But, like Mamma told Sister Johnson, *"I just have to find a way to make him happy, to really please him and then he'll love me. It's my fault, not his. He's under a lot of stress,"* I convinced myself.

Thinking back, I made excuse after excuse for him – for them. How could I have been so blind? I guess when you're broken, you filter everything through that brokenness and it comes out polluted. I was deceived at my own will.

One day I went to his apartment and knocked on the door, but there was no answer. His car was in the parking lot, so I thought maybe he was sleeping. I went to his bedroom window, with my fist poised to knock when I heard voices. I put my ear to the window, only to discover he was with another woman. I wasn't shocked, but I was surprised that it hurt so deeply. You would have thought I would be use to this by now. "Why am I not good enough for anybody? Why can't I ever do anything right? What's wrong with me?"

Once again, broken hearted, I went back to my dorm room. He called a few hours later and told me he was coming to pick me up. I contemplated confronting him, but what good would it have done? He would have either lied about it or beat me again.

I waited for him for hours, but he never showed up. Early the next morning I was awakened by the phone ringing. Marlon was calling me from jail. It was his third strike, there would be no bond. He had already been to prison twice on drug related charges. I knew he was going to do time, and I was right. He was sentenced to twenty years.

I was devastated. What would I do without him? I *"loved"* him so much. Suddenly, I was confronted with an even bigger issue. With Marlon in jail, I no longer had anyone to supply the drugs I craved. What kind of person am I? Here the man I love is facing twenty years in prison and all I'm thinking about is where I was going to get my next high. Such selfishness, but that's who you become when you're an addict.

Immediately, the same thoughts that now had become familiar replayed like a bad record. *'Do it, do it right now! Don't wait. It won't hurt and you won't have to deal with the pain anymore. Do the world a favor, Angel. You've done too much. It's too late. There's no hope for people like you. Do it!!!'* It was getting harder and harder to ignore the thoughts.

CHAPTER 12

They say hind sight is 20/20. I wish I understood that it was actually the hand of God that intervened and severed the toxic relationships in my life. Believe it or not, at the time of each and every breakup, I actually prayed and asked God to bring them back and was angry with Him when He didn't. I'm so glad God didn't answer all of my prayers with a "Yes."

After Marlon, I decided it was time to cure my addiction, but how? I needed to do some research, so I went to the library to use a computer, but they were in short supply. "Good Morning, I didn't reserve a computer, but was hoping one would be available since it's still early."

"You do know a reservation is required, right?" The frumpy old woman looked at me over the rim of her black rimmed glasses.

"Yes Ma'am, I do. I was just hoping one was available."

"Yes, there is one available. I suppose you can use it,

but you'll have to be done in thirty minutes. Someone else followed the rules and reserved it ahead of time."

"Yes Ma'am. Thank you."

"Mrs. Frumpy," escorted me to the computer and I began the task of finding an outpatient treatment center off campus. No one at the University needed to know my business. My scholarships would be in jeopardy. I found a place, however, it was almost two hours away, but I was desperate. I was already beginning to crave the poison.

I jotted down the number and returned to my dorm room. I put the key in the door, opened it, and was startled by my roommate, Iverem. Great, now she wants to come home. "Hi my friend," she said hugging me.

"Hi there Iverem, you're home."

"I am. My boyfriend and I broke up, so it looks like this will be home again for me. Will you help me get my stuff out my car?"

"Sure," I said throwing my back pack on the bed. We made three trips to her car, lugging large boxes up the steps each time.

"This dorm needs an elevator!" Iverem fussed in her Nigerian accent.

I needed to make my call, but of course I couldn't with her in the room. So I helped her unpack, and I have to say, I was grateful for the distraction from the craziness in my world. We talked about her home and how much she missed her family.

Iverem had a strength I admired and maybe even envied. What courage it must have taken for her to come to a new country into a new culture where she knew no one.

"You're so strong Iverem. I don't know if I could do what you've done."

"What do you mean?"

"You left everyone you loved and everything that was familiar just for an education."

"It was my privilege and duty. Many women in my country don't get such an opportunity. So I must work hard so I can go back and make a difference." She spoke of how her family valued education and how she wanted help them financially. "Well, I have to go to class, but I'll see you later Angel."

"Okay Iverem, see you later."

"Oh, by the way, thanks so much for helping me with my things, I appreciate it."

"Not a problem, see you later."

As soon as she closed the door, I rushed to the phone and nervously dialed the number. "Good morning, New Start Treatment Center, how may I help you?"

"Uhhh, I have...I have a friend that wants to break her drug habit and I was calling to get some information about your treatment program."

"Not a problem, let me transfer you to one of our counselors, they can answer your questions. Is that okay?"

"Sure, that's fine. Thank you."

She placed me on a brief hold. "Good morning, this is Mrs. Roland. How may I help you today?"

"Uh, good morning Mrs. Roland, I have a friend that wants to get off drugs. I'm calling to get some information about your program."

"I'm happy to help. What's your friend's drug of choice?"

"Cocaine."

"What form does she take it?"

"She usually snorts it, but she has freebased too."

"Well, let me tell you a little bit about our program. It is out patient, but it does require an initial thirty day stay. Once you successfully complete the thirty day program, we assign an Accountability Sponsor to you. At that time, you have to attend meetings every evening for the first four weeks. After which, we complete an assessment to determine how you are progressing. Any questions?"

"No Ma'am. It's just that…well, my friend's in school and she can't stay for thirty days."

"I understand, but it is a requirement. It takes about two weeks just to get the drug out of your system. Maybe she can speak with her counselor at school to see if some arrangements can be made so she can catch up on her assignments. Where there's a will, there's a way."

"Well, thanks for your help. I'll let my friend know."

"You're very welcome. Please, let your friend know she can call and speak with one of our counselors anytime, day or night, okay?"

"Yes Ma'am." I hung up the phone trying to think of a way to leave school for thirty days. I couldn't dare tell my Counselor or Dean the truth. This was yet another thing I decided I would have to do alone. I grew up knowing how to keep secrets and not telling anyone about family business. So isolating myself wasn't hard for me at all. This was definitely a time I missed my friendship with Carmen.

I concocted a lie and made an appointment with the Dean. "Hello Mr. Matthews, how are you today?

"Well I'm doing quite well Ms. Sanders. How may I help you?"

"Well, it's…it's my dad. He has cancer and he has to have surgery." I turned on the water works. "My Mom passed years ago, so I just have to be there to take care of him when he's released from the hospital, he doesn't have anyone else. I would only be out a couple of weeks, but I'm concerned about my classes."

Mr. Matthews handed me a tissue, "I am so sorry to hear that."

Bless his heart; he was genuinely concerned about me. "It's a very noble thing you're doing, Ms. Sanders. Children don't honor their parents like that anymore. No, don't you worry about a thing I'll take care of everything. I'll speak with your instructors and you'll be allowed to make up your work. You have enough to worry about with your dad. Are you sure two weeks is going to be enough?"

"Two weeks is plenty. Thank you so much Mr. Matthews, that's a load off my mind."

"Not a problem at all, glad to help. You and your dad are in my prayers. You let me know if there's anything further I can do for you, Angel."

"Yes Sir, thanks again, I really appreciate you." He escorted me to the door and gave me a reassuring pat on the shoulder. I could have won an award for my performance. I hated myself for taking advantage of Mr. Matthews' kindness, but I would have done it again rather than tell the truth, which at that point was becoming harder and harder to do. You can lie so long, that you forget the truth yourself.

Iverem was a bit of a germophobe, which worked to my advantage. I told her that I had come down with the mumps. She packed her things and got out of that dorm room faster than a toupee flies in a hurricane. She agreed to room with one of the other girls in the dorm for not two, but three weeks.

I called Mrs. Roland back at New Start to inquire about the symptoms of withdrawal. Of course, she knew there was never a "friend," but she never condemned me. She simply gave me the information, honestly and directly. "The cravings will become increasingly stronger, depending on how heavy you…I mean, your friend used. Withdrawal can last a couple of days to a week."

"She will deal with anxiety and have trouble sleeping. After the initial symptoms subside, she will probably deal with depression. My advice is that she not try to do this alone. She needs to be under a doctor's care. May I give you the name of some of the centers?"

"Sure, that would be great."

Mrs. Rowland gave me the name of four centers, but they were all too close to the University. I couldn't risk anybody discovering my dirty little secret, so I did it alone, as usual. Both the physical and mental symptoms were excruciating for the first 48 hours, and I had trouble sleeping for a few weeks. It was all worth it to finally get the poison out of my system. I wondered how much damage I had done to my body and I how long the freedom would last.

After the three weeks and lots of disinfectant, Iverem moved back into the room. We still lived our separate lives, but it was good to have the company. With Marlon out of my life and the drugs too, I was back on track... well, as much as possible anyway. My focus was making excellent grades and working.

CHAPTER 13

I was at my desk studying for an exam when the phone rang. The voice on the other end was Uncle Keith. His voice sounded like sanity. I was basking in that sanity when he said, "Angel, did you hear me? Are you still there?"

"Oh, yeah…I mean, yes Sir, I'm here."

"Alex and I are coming down to see you next weekend and I'm bringing my other favorite girl with me. I can't wait for you to meet her. I told her all about you. How well you're doing in school and how very proud I am of you."

I was so ashamed of the life I was living and the lies I had kept. "Oh, Uncle Keith, believe me, there's nothing great about me, but I can't wait to meet her."

"What'cha talk'n about sweetheart, I brag on you all the time. Now listen, I'm gonna need you to give me the names of a few hotels close to the University. We're coming in on Friday morning and we're gonna stay until Monday, so we even get to visit your church."

"Church?! Uncle Keith, I ahhh, really haven't joined a church yet." *What in the world am I going to do about church?'* I thought.

"That's okay; we'll just go to the one you're visiting. It's going to be so good to see you. Alex and I miss you so much. But I'm kinda sensing some tension between you and your dad. Are you two alright?"

"What makes you say that?"

"Well, I just knew he would be excited about coming with us, but he flat out refused."

"It's just the normal father/daughter disagreements – nothing serious, Uncle Keith, really."

"We're gonna talk a little more when I get there, but don't forget to call me with the names of the hotels. I love you Angel, I'll talk to you soon."

"Love you too Uncle Keith, I can't wait to see you and Alex."

I only had one class on Fridays – Chemistry from 8 to 10 a.m. and Uncle Keith said they should be pulling into the campus at about 10:30 or 11:00. After class I raced to the dorm and couldn't stop looking out the window. At 11am on the dot, I spotted them pulling into one of the parking spaces next to my building.

I ran down the hall and three flights of stairs feeling like a kid at Christmas. Uncle Keith and Alex flung open the car doors and rushed to greet me. Alex had gotten so tall and even more handsome. He must have grown six inches since I had last seen him. Uncle Keith's hug was all I needed and I held on tight. "Hey Angel, I've got someone I want you to meet."

"Angel, this is Hope." I turned my attention to his girlfriend and extended my hand politely.

"Hi, I'm Angel, so glad to meet you." She was absolutely gorgeous, standing about 5'8", medium build, with long hair neatly pulled back into a ponytail. Her skin was flawless. Her eyes were full of wisdom beyond her years. She had the kind of eyes that could look right through you.

Hope took my hand, pulled me into her arms and embraced me like she knew me. "Angel, it's an honor and privilege to meet you. Your uncle talks about you so much and God has had you on my heart for quite some time. I've been praying for you." Her words were authentic and full of love. But, how can that be? She just met me. If she knew me, she would know there was nothing to love.

"Thank you Ms. Hope, and thank you for your prayers; I need all the prayers I can get." I tried to laugh it off, but her words were still resonating in my heart.

"Hey Angel, can we see your room?" Alex said anxiously.

"Sure little brother, whose not so little anymore," I said putting him in a head lock. "Alex, you've grown like a weed!"

"Yep, I'm way taller than you now."

"And what's with the bass I hear in your voice. What a handsome dude you are."

Alex grabbed my hand and pulled me toward the dorm. He put his arm around my neck and whispered, "It's okay Angel, now I can protect you."

"I believe you can Alex – I believe you can," I smiled.

I opened the door to my well-manicured dorm room, knowing I had Alex's approval when he said, "This is so cool!"

"You like it Alex?"

"Yeah, it's like your own apartment. Who's bed is this?" he said pointing to Iverem's bed.

"It's my roommate, that's her side of the room."

"Is she from Africa?"

"Yep, she is."

"Oh, cool. I can tell from her stuff."

"Angel, I'm so proud of you, this is beautiful." Uncle Keith said, walking over to my desk. "Look Hope, this is where she makes those "A's."

Everything in me wished I was worthy of Uncle Keith's compliments. "Hey, who's hungry?" I changed the subject.

"I could use a bite to eat," Hope said graciously.

"What do you guys feel like eating?" I asked.

"You know me I'll eat just about anything," Uncle Keith confessed.

"How about Mexican food?" Alex interjected.

"Great idea Alex, I know a great little place not far from campus. Me and uh…uh, a friend have eaten there a couple of times." I was praying Hope didn't pick up on the pause in my sentence. Though I think she did because she looked at me and smiled knowingly.

We all piled into the car and headed to the restaurant. The food was excellent, but the conversation and company even better. I hadn't laughed that much in months. Having them all there was priceless. It eased the thoughts and the pain locked in my heart. The fear of using again was my constant companion day and night.

"So Angel, what church have you been attending and what time does it start, we don't wanna be late." Uncle Keith asked eagerly.

"Uh, well, Uncle Keith, to tell you the truth I really haven't uh, been to church in a while. You see I've been so busy with school and all."

"Angel! What do you mean you've been too busy?" I could hear the disappointment in his voice.

"Well," Hope said softly, "I'm sure there are plenty of churches around here. Why don't we allow the Lord to lead us to the one He wants us to attend?"

As Hope was speaking she gently placed her hand on Uncle Keith's hand and looked at him. "Hey, that's a good idea Ms. Hope," Alex agreed.

"It looks like I'm out numbered. We'll scope out the area on our way back to the school."

I wanted to say thanks, but just smiled at her instead. We did some shopping before heading back to the University and by the time we made it back to campus the sun was just beginning to set. "Angel, can you show us around campus?" Alex pleaded.

"Hey, good idea Alex," Ms. Hope agreed. "I heard there's a really nice Prayer Garden on campus."

"Yes, everyone says it's really beautiful."

"You've never been?" Surprised, Uncle Keith asked.

"Nope, not yet Uncle Keith, you know – very busy, school, studying, and work."

Again, Ms. Hope to the rescue, "Well, we'll all get to experience it for the first time."

I hadn't seen flowers that beautiful since my Grandma's garden. Roses, Mums, Tulips, and a deep purple flower I had never seen before. The fragrance captured your senses immediately and there was a crystal stream that ran though the Garden, which fed a small, but grand waterfall. The soft sound of the trickling water and the incredible sunset was the very definition of tranquility.

"This is incredible. The perfect balance of beauty, sweet aromas, and peace, just takes your breath away," Hope said poetically.

Uncle Keith took Ms. Hope's hand as he looked into those deep eyes of hers and said, "Your beauty takes my breath away Hope, both inside and out."

Alex and I look at each other and smiled. "I am so grateful to God for bringing you into my life." He lowered himself to one knee, "Hope, I love and respect you and would be so honored if you would be my wife."

Uncle Keith pulled the most beautiful ring out of his pocket and presented it to Ms. Hope. "Oh, thank you Lord! Yes!!! Yes, of course! I would be honored to by your wife!!!"

The scene was like something right out of one of those perfect boy meets girl romantic movies. I was so very happy for them. "Way to go Uncle Keith!"

Uncle Keith winked his eye and Alex returned the gesture. "Wait a minute, Alex did you know Uncle Keith was going to propose?" "It's a guy thing, you wouldn't understand," they both agreed. We all broke into laughter and enjoyed the moment. How special it was for Uncle Keith to wait to propose so I could be there. Ms. Hope was getting an incredible man and Uncle Keith seemed to be getting a pretty amazing woman.

The weekend flew by and the Sunday morning sun was staring me in the face. What in the world will I even wear to church? I got up and looked though my closet for any possible choices. Then the thought occurred to me, maybe Iverem had something I could wear. She gave me her blessing to go through her closet and chose anything I wanted. I found a cute multi-colored dress with a full skirt. "This looks like it should fit."

When I tried it on and I must say I looked pretty good in it. "Ding, ding, ding – we have a winner!" I said as I admired myself in the mirror. With that problem solved, I hopped in the shower, did my hair and threw on a little make up. I knew Uncle Keith would be on time.

We decided on a small church just five blocks from campus called, "Redemption Church." The sign read: Service Starts at 10:00 a.m., and at 9:40 on the dot they were pulling up to my dorm. We were walking in the church at 9:53. "Excellent, we're on time," Uncle Keith said looking at his watch.

"Honey let's sit near the front," Hope suggested.

"Sure Baby," he agreed.

'Uggggbh!' I wanted to sit on the back row in the last seat. I hadn't been to church since shortly after Momma's funeral.

Several people came to greet us and shake our hands. "Welcome to Redemption Church, glad to have you."

"Thank you," Uncle Keith and Ms. Hope said politely.

"This sure is a friendly church," Alex added his opinion.

"This is my niece, Angel. She's here attending the University."

'Gee, thanks Uncle Keith!' The silver haired dignified lady extended her hand to me. I reluctantly shook it and tried to muster up some graciousness. "So, you attend the University?" The church lady repeated.

"Yes, Ma'am."

"Well, we would love to be your church home away from home."

"We'll see," I said smiling while thinking, *'Lady, after today you will never see me again!'*

Within a few minutes the musicians mounted their instruments and began to play. The silver haired lady was helped onto the platform and given a mic. "Good morning Saints!" she began. "I have been praying for a move of God all week in this service and I believe all God wants this morning is our *"Yes,"* and He will have His way."

I just sat there, defiant, rehearsing every time God failed me, or so I thought He failed me. The silver haired lady began to pray as the musicians played softly. She worshipped and praised God, thanking Him for how He had brought her through time and time again. She praised Him for never giving up on her when she was determined not to live for Him. She thanked Him for saving her and healing her. Then thanked Him for delivering her from drugs.

You could have bought me for a penny. *That sweet little church lady…on drugs!!! What?!!!'*

She continued. "Lord, thank You for your mercy that's new every single morning. Thank You for Your loving kindness that is better than life." Then she sang Momma's favorite song.

As she began the chorus, I excused myself and hurried to the ladies room. I stood in the mirror and those same old thoughts began again. *"You feel the love of God?? Ha!!! Girl with all you've done – you know He can't possibly love you. Look at you, in this church trying to pretend you're somebody. Hasn't life taught you who you are? Some people are born for this stuff, not you Angel. God has given up on you so stop hoping."*

Just then, the door opened. "Hey, Angel its Ms. Hope. Ha, nature calls at the craziest times, right?"

"God loves you so much Angel. It doesn't matter what you've done, God can, will, and wants to forgive you. All you need to do is repent and ask."

"Oh…yeah…right. I know Ms. Hope, but I'm good," I said turning to walk out of the bathroom.

The thoughts were loud and got louder the more I agreed with them. They were so loud I couldn't hear anything else until the service was over. "Wasn't that a good Word, Angel?" Uncle Keith asked excitedly.

"Huh…oh, yeah…yeah, it was really good." I hadn't heard a word of the sermon. I chose not to hear.

We stopped at a restaurant near their hotel for dinner after the service. "You're quiet Angel, are you okay?"

"Sure Alex, I'm fine, just thinking of all I have to do this week. You know exams and stuff."

"College must be hard."

"Oh Alex, it is a lot of work, but I really like it. You're going to do very well when you go to college."

"You think so?"

"Absolutely!" I said locking my arm with his.

We were all stuffed when we left the restaurant, rather than going back to the dorm, I decided to hang out in their hotel room and watch a movie. Spending every moment I could with them was important to me. Early Monday morning, Uncle Keith, Alex and Ms. Hope were waiting outside to say goodbye. I threw on my robe and headed downstairs. "There she is my beautiful niece. I'm sure going to miss you Princess."

"Oh, I'm gonna miss you too Uncle Keith," he said as he gave me one of his famous bear hugs and kissed me on my forehead.

"Hey Angel, I'm gonna miss you too – every day." Alex reassured. "But I'm okay; I don't want you to worry." When I hugged him, he whispered, "Daddy is not so bad anymore, so please, don't worry."

"I'll try not to Alex."

"It was such a pleasure to meet you my dear. Anytime you need anything, just give me a call. Your Uncle will give you my number."

"I'm so happy for you both. Thank you Ms. Hope, for everything."

One more hug from Uncle Keith as he handed me a card. I watched sadly as they drove down the drive that fed into the main road. Alex waved until they were out of sight. Slowly, I turned and walked back to my room. I laid the envelope on my desk, changed clothes, watched a little television, and then decided to go back to bed until my class began at 1:00pm.

As I dozed off, I remembered the envelope. It read:

My Dear Angel,

I know there are bad feelings between you and your dad. You haven't volunteered any information and I have to respect that. But I want you to know, I am always here for you, no matter what. You and Alex mean the world to me and I need you to believe that.

Here's a couple hundred dollars, go do something special for yourself, you know, the girly stuff you ladies do.

Tons of love,

Uncle Keith

I smiled, replaying the weekend over in my head, especially church. Even though my soul was dark and barren, somewhere in the remotest part there lay a tiny bit of hope. It was the only thing keeping me alive.

CHAPTER 14

Before I knew it, my freshman year was over and I finished with a 3.75 GPA. Instead of going home for the summer, I took summer courses and worked at the library. A new addition had been recently added and they were doing some major shifting and rearranging. They needed help and I gladly accepted the offer. I certainly wasn't going back to that house. Besides, now that Uncle Keith was getting married, he cut back on his monthly allowance.

On my way back for lunch I stopped to check the mail. There was a credit card advertisement, an overdue book notice from the University library, a coupon for two dollars off a large pizza, and a letter. I trembled when I saw the return address:

Inmate Marlon Simpson

SPN: 5555666

Department of Corrections

I ran back to my dorm room and threw the letter on my desk and paced back and forth trying to figure out what to do. I was consumed by fear. It was as if he was actually in the room with me. I was startled when the phone rang. "Hello."

"Well, hello my dear, it's Sister Johnson." My fears were immediately quieted just by the sound of her voice.

"Hi Sister Johnson, how are you? You don't know how good it is to hear your voice."

"It's good to hears yours too Princess, how you doing?"

"I'm fine, just trying to enjoy the summer."

"Well, you know your mother had high hopes for you. I know she's smiling down from Heaven. You make us all proud, Angel." We talked until it was time for me to go to class. On my way out the door I tore the letter up and gave it a proper burial. I flushed it along with him down the toilet.

As my sophomore year began, the planning for Uncle Keith and Ms. Hope's wedding was in full swing. She called and asked if I wanted to go shopping with her for her wedding dress, of course I agreed. I couldn't believe she wanted to include me in such an important task. She picked me up from school that Friday after I got off work and I stayed with her overnight. Of course, I lied and said I had to work Sunday to avoid the whole church scene again.

Ms. Hope's apartment was very neat and clean and the atmosphere was so peaceful. Her walls were painted soft lavender and there were fresh flowers in every room. I suspected Uncle Keith had something to do with that. She had tons and tons of books on shelves. Many were on prayer, worship and different Bible Studies. I wondered if she had read them all.

She showed me to my room which was very girly. The comforter, pillows and curtains all matched. Everything was pink with sparkly accents. Once I got settled, she gently knocked on the door, "Angel, you ready?"

"Sure, coming."

We sat at her dining room table where she had a large wedding planning book, magazines, and fabric swatches all spread out. I was very uncomfortable with her. It seemed like she could see right through me. I had a strange feeling that she knew all my secrets. I'm not sure why, but that's how I felt.

"Some of the bridesmaids are coming over. We'll make it a girl's night," she said sounding like a school girl.

"Sounds good to me," I agreed, but wondered if I'd fit in or be comfortable around them.

"Angel, Keith and I were talking and we thought it would be wonderful if you were in the wedding. I would love it if you would be one of my bridesmaids."

I couldn't say no to Uncle Keith. "Oh, that's so sweet. Thank you, I would be honored."

While we were looking at swatches and her ideas for flowers, the doorbell rang. It was the other three bridesmaids. They were all excited and greeted one another. "Ladies, I have someone I want you to meet. This is my soon to be niece, Angel."

"Hello everyone," I said shyly.

"Well ladies, I have snacks of course and I made us some virgin Pina Coladas! Let's get busy!"

We sat around the dining room table chatting, exchanging ideas and making suggestions. To my surprise the evening actually turned out well. After all the ladies left I helped clean the kitchen and tidy up a bit. "So, did you have a good time Angel?"

"Yes, I really did."

"Great, I'm so glad you did. Well, I know you're tired and I am too – you wanna call it a night?"

"Sure."

"Okay, well, let's pray."

"Pray?"

"Yes, I always pray with my guests before we go to bed…house rule!"

Without waiting for my approval, she took my hand and started to pray…

"Father, I am so very grateful to You for all You're doing. You know the plans You have for us, plans for good and not for evil, to give us an expected future and a hope. I submit to and embrace every plan and purpose You have for our lives even when I don't understand. Your ways are higher than my ways and Your thoughts are higher than my thoughts."

"Lord, thank You for Angel. I pray You continue to watch over her and I decree every plan and purpose You have for her life shall come to fruition. I pray that Your peace, Father, will guard her heart and mind through Christ Jesus. I thank You Father that Your angels are protecting us and ask You for sweet sleep, in Jesus name. Amen."

After her powerful prayer, I went into the room and closed the door, but could hear her praying in her room just like Momma used to do.

I usually had trouble sleeping when I was away from home, but that night I slept like a baby. I awoke to a gentle knock on the door. "Good morning Dear, you better get showered and dressed, we've got a long day ahead of us."

As I was combing my hair I could smell bacon cooking. It's funny how certain scents can take you back to a place and time. At that moment I was back in Momma's kitchen, so I closed my eyes and enjoyed the memory.

After I made the bed I hurried to the kitchen to see if I could do anything to help. "Did you sleep well Angel?"

"Yes Ma'am, I did."

"Good, good."

"Can I help with anything?"

"Sure, will you grab a couple of glasses from the cabinet on the left and get the pitcher of orange juice out the fridge?"

"Yes Ma'am."

The table she set was gorgeous. There were sunflowers in a crystal vase that glistened as it caught the rays of the morning sun. The dishes looked expensive. They were white with a purple and silver band around the edges. There were purple linen napkins with silver napkin rings. The water goblets had a soft lavender tint and there were juice glasses next to each one. "Everything is so pretty Ms. Hope. Is somebody special coming for breakfast?"

"Absolutely…you!"

"All of this for me? I sure hope I don't break anything. I'm famous for messing things up you know."

"No, I don't know, and guess what, if something breaks the world as we know it won't cease to exist. So relax. Now, let's say grace and have some breakfast."

After the dishes were done, we made a list of errands and were on our way. We made stops at the dry cleaners and the florist before heading to the bridal shop. Her appointment was at 11:00 a.m., and the ladies from last night met us there.

The bridal consultant had a Southern drawl like I had never heard. "Well, hello y'all, my name is Sam, short for Samantha. I have the pleasure of assist'n y'all today. Now, let me guess, you are the blush'n bride, rite?" she said pointing to Ms. Hope.

"Yes, I am. How could you tell?"

"Well Darl'n you're just a-glowing all over. He must be a mighty fine young man."

"Oh, he absolutely is," Ms. Hope said blushing.

"Well ladies, let's git this party started. Now Bride, tell me a lil' bit 'bout your style – you know, your taste, what you like."

Fifteen minutes later, Sam came back with an arm full of gowns. "I think these will do nicely. But, I especially like this one. So let's start with it first, shall we?"

"It's so beautiful," Ms. Hope glowed.

"Isn't it jus to die for? Now, go on in and try it on Darl'n. We just can't wait to see it on ya Hun."

When Ms. Hope emerged from the dressing room we were all amazed. The dress was simple, but very elegant. It was an off the shoulder, champagne colored dress that fit her perfectly. The entire dress was covered in an understated Italian lace.

It had a wide gross grain ribbon belt at the waist that was studded with crystals, which simply tied in the back. It plunged to a soft scooped back and cascaded down to a small train that flowed across the floor as she walked – it was perfect! "I think this is the one!" She said admiring the dress in the mirror.

"I believe you jus' may be rite. But hol' yer' horses, we got a ton of dresses to try on Darl'n."

After a solid two hours of trying on dresses, Ms. Hope chose the very first one. What a wonderful time I had with the ladies. After a wonderful day of watching Ms. Hope try on many, and I mean many gowns, we all went to lunch, and then she took me back to my dorm. "Thank you so much Angel, I had such a great time with you."

"No – thank you. I really enjoyed you as well and thanks for making everything so special."

"You are special Angel."

Jan Davis

CHAPTER 15

One year later, the big day finally arrived. I was so excited for them I could hardly stand it. Uncle Keith and now, my soon to be Aunt Hope picked me up Thursday night and I stayed with her to help out with any last minute details. On Friday we got pedicures and manicures. The florist was our final stop before heading to the wedding rehearsal and dinner.

Ms. Hope chose simple lavender roses and purple orchids for her bouquet with pops of silver ribbon. She really loved purple. The maid's bouquets were beautifully understated as well. I never thought purple and silver would look good together, but it was gorgeous.

The wedding planner, Brittany, was absolutely amazing. She anticipated Ms. Hope's every need. Saturday morning, she sent a white limousine to drive us to the hair salon. The beautician placed Ms. Hope's hair in an up-do adding crystal pins that attached her long veil. The driver waited outside of the salon like we were celebrities, then chauffeured us to our final destination.

After a twenty minute ride, we arrived at the venue. The driver to pulled around to the porta cache' where Brittany awaited. The ceremony was to be held in the Chapel, which included an elaborate bridal suite. The bridal suite was something to behold. Fragrant lavender roses filled vases on a marble makeup counter. Three plush leather sofas arranged in a square formed a cozy lounge area. In the center was a large mirrored table topped with snacks, fruit, and a variety of beverages.

I remember asking Uncle Keith about Ms. Hope's parents. He told me she was adopted when she was a baby and unfortunately, her adopted mother had passed several years ago. So when an older elegantly dressed woman walked into the bridal suite, I wondered who she was. When Ms. Hope saw her, she ran to meet her and they embraced. The other ladies whispered, "Angel, do you know who she is?"

"No, I don't. I've never seen her before."

Ms. Hope must have heard us because she broke their embrace and said, "Hey everyone, I want you all to meet my birth mother, Katherine Miles."

We were all stunned. "I have been searching for her for years and finally found her a few months ago. I sent her a letter, she called me and I invited her to our wedding and she's here! All the way from Seattle."

"Hello everyone, I'm so very pleased to meet you, but nothing is more precious than seeing you Hope."

After greeting her we made our exit. This was a special moment and we wanted to give them some privacy. "It was so very hard to let you go Hope, but I loved you and wanted to do what was best for you. I was in no shape to raise a child. I was a mess back then. I know it's your special day, and it's hard, but can you ever forgive me for what I've done?"

"It's wasn't hard at all. "I already have. I'm so thankful that you're here," they embraced.

Ms. Hope called us all back into the bridal suite and shared how special her Mom was and that her being there was an answer to prayers she had prayed for years. There wasn't a dry eye in the room. Even Brittany was crying.

"Brittany, can you go and find my Dad, I want him to meet my birth mother."

"Done," Brittany said as she walked out the room.

We hugged Ms. Katherine and were amazed at how loving Ms. Hope was toward her. A few minutes later, her Dad walked in. When he looked at his daughter tears instantly filled his eyes. "You look so beautiful, Sweetheart. If your Mom could see you now…"

"I'm sure she can, daddy. I know she's watching from Heaven. Daddy, I have someone I want you to meet. This is Ms. Katherine Miles, my birth Mother."

He was shocked momentarily, but gathered himself, extended his hand, and smiled. "Thank you so much Katherine for bringing her into the world. She has been such a blessing to me and her mother."

"It is I who thank you and your wife for adopting her, loving her and grooming her to be the lovely young woman she is today."

This was how forgiveness was supposed to look.

This is how honor looked. I had never seen anything like it before. There was no trace of bitterness, hatred or jealousy. How do they do it? I couldn't and wouldn't ever forgive my daddy for the things he had done to me.

"Okay everyone, I just came from the groom's suite and they are all just about ready. We have thirty minutes until show time. Ms. Katherine, I have a gentleman outside who will escort you to your seat," Brittany instructed.

"Thank you my dear, I appreciate it." Ms. Hope gave her one more hug and a kiss on the cheek, then Brittany took her hand and walked her out.

"Well, I guess I'd better join the guys, but I'll be waiting for you sweetheart. I've been waiting all your life to take this bitter-sweet walk down the aisle with you on my arm. Keith loves you. He's a good and honorable man Hope. I know he's going to take great care of you," her Dad said as he kissed her on the forehead.

This was all so foreign to me. You don't know how dysfunctional you really are until you finally see functional. While they were finishing up I slipped out quickly to go to the groom's suite. I had to see Uncle Keith and Alex before the ceremony began. I knocked softly on the door. "Come in."

"It's me Uncle Keith. Is everyone decent?"

"The coast is clear. Come on in Angel."

They all looked so handsome. "Hey Sis, you clean up pretty good," Alex nudged me jokingly. "Doesn't she look beautiful?"

"Yes she does." Uncle Keith agreed.

"You guys look pretty amazing yourselves.

"How's my bride-to-be?"

"She's pretty amazing Uncle Keith. Did you know her birth mother is here?"

"So she did come? I was praying she would. When Hope told me she invited her – well, I just didn't want her to be disappointed, especially today."

"It was the most incredible thing I've ever seen. Ms. Hope, her Dad and Ms. Katherine embraced one another and it was really genuine. It was...well... peaceful and sweet."

"That's how God does things Angel, when you give Him your, "*Yes*.""

"Well, I've gotta get back, it's almost time." Uncle Keith kissed my cheek then I hurried back to the bridal suite.

The wedding was perfect. There was so much love in her Dad's eyes as he walked her down the aisle. Uncle Keith stood noble and honorable, beholding the beauty of his bride.

After pictures the bridal party headed to the reception. With all that was going on I forgot it would be the first time I would see daddy since he did what he did to me. Just the thought of it made me physically ill.

As soon as we entered the venue I spotted him sitting at a table in the back by himself. He was evil personified. The longer I sat and watched him the more hatred flooded my heart. Then, I saw her...it *was* her! It was the lady from Momma's funeral. Only this time she wasn't wearing the black dress and big church lady hat. *'I knew it; she does look just like daddy!'*

I could tell by the look on his face when she walked in he was surprised to see her. They talked for a few minutes then he walked away. She sat down looking disappointed by his response. Now was my chance to find out who she was. I made my way to the table. "Who are you? You were at my Momma's funeral, now you're at my uncle's wedding. Who are you?" I demanded.

"Angel!"

"How do you know my name?"

"I'll tell you – I'll tell you everything," she whispered.

"We can talk in the bridal suite, just through those doors, then to the left." I followed closely behind so she wouldn't have a chance to get away from me this time.

We walked into the bridal suite and I closed the door behind us. "Now, who are you?"

"My name is Joan. Joan Sanders, I'm your father's twin sister."

"Twin sister? But he only had five brothers?"

"No, we only had one brother, Leon."

"Is that the brother that was killed?

"Yes. Please sit down, I'll tell you everything. You deserve to know."

"Our daddy, Leon Sr., was a hardworking man, but he was an alcoholic and had a horrible temper. Our mother, Nora, was the object of his anger. Oh, my goodness, they fought something awful. Most of the fights would start because mother loved the taverns and bars. She also loved men – lots and lots of men."

"I can't imagine having to live with a terrible father and mother."

"It was terrible. One day, me, Leon Jr., and John, your daddy, came home from school and heard noises coming from mother and daddy's bedroom. We thought they were fighting again, so we burst through the door to try to stop it. It wasn't daddy on top of mother; it was one of daddy's friends. He cursed at us and told us to get out and close the door. Mother laughed and said, "Y'all kids go on in yo room, momma's handling business with Mr. Ray right now."

"I had never seen that look in John's eyes before. He hated mother. He was so angry that he went and got daddy's gun. Leon Jr. tried to stop him, they struggled and that's when..." her eyes filled with tears. "...that's when the gun went off and Leon Jr. fell to the floor. Mother and Ray, came running from the bedroom. She started screaming and Ray, being the coward that he was, grabbed his clothes and ran out the house. Leon Jr. was dead. John fell to his knees beside his lifeless body and cried the bitterest tears I had ever seen."

"Oh my goodness, how horrible!" I gasped as she continued her story.

"Mother yelled, "Look at what you did boy. You killed yo brother! You killed yo brother!" Then she grabbed us both, slapped us and told us to stop crying and then threw us on the sofa."

"This is what you both are gonna say happened if

you don't want to rot in jail for the rest of your lives, you hear me!"

"She made us lie and say Leon Jr. found daddy's gun and was playing with it when it went off and he accidently shot himself. John and I were terrified. When the police came, that's what we told them. We told the same lie to daddy and we've been lying ever since."

"Poor daddy, he grieved to death. He blamed himself for having the gun in the house. But of course, it wasn't his fault. Times were hard for black people back then. He wanted to make sure we were all protected."

"Even after daddy's funeral, Mother still brought man after man into our home. Some would beat us, they cursed us, and some even molested me, but she didn't care. I saw John's hatred for Mother grow every day. I saw a hatred in him towards me begin to grow as well."

I couldn't believe what I as hearing, but it made perfect sense. That's why daddy was the way he was. "But I don't understand, why did he hate you?"

"I think he just hated women period. As a young man he drank heavily like our daddy and isolated himself. When he got old enough he joined the Army for a while, but received a dishonorable discharge for intoxication and insubordination. After that he couldn't keep a job for years."

"Then he met your mother. She was a good God fearing woman. She prayed for him all the time, but I knew he wasn't good for her. I begged her to leave him alone and go her way, but he said she loved him. When he found out I told her to leave him, he cursed me and told me he never wanted to see me again. He said I was just like Mother and to a degree, he was right. I was in the bars, sleeping around with man after man. Married, single, it didn't matter. I just wanted to be loved, you know. Everybody wants to be loved," she began to cry.

I believe she had cried those same tears for years. "What happened to your mother...my grandmother?"

"She died in 1977. She had a heart attack. John didn't even come to the funeral."

We sat in silence for what seemed like an hour. "Well Angel, I'm so sorry we had to meet like this. I just found John again, right before your Momma passed and I've been trying to make amends ever since, but he won't hear me."

"John was such a good boy, but he got that temper from daddy. He just keeps closing me out. Unforgiveness and bitterness has eaten him away like cancer. He's mean and hateful – I can see it in his eyes"

"Oh, you don't know how mean and hateful he is."

"I know child, but I hope you can find it in your heart to forgive him, now that you know the truth."

"The truth doesn't excuse him for all he's done!"

"I understand. I'll say this and I'll go on my way. Take a long look at your daddy Angel, because that's exactly what you will become in twenty years if you chose not to forgive." She hugged me and left. I sat there with her words cutting me to my core.

When the reception was over Uncle Keith and Aunt Hope left for their honeymoon, so one of the bridesmaids took me back to school. After talking to Aunt Joan I had so much to process.

Sister Johnson once told me brokenness and dysfunction is a cycle that visits generation after generation until someone decides enough is enough and with the help of God, He helps them break it.

I had experienced the extremes of both forgiveness and un-forgiveness in one emotionally charged day. I think I knew deep down, somewhere inside me, I needed to forgive.

What un-forgiveness does to you is a horrible thing. Much worse than what the person you're holding in un-forgiveness did because now, you're violated twice. But *how* to forgive escaped me. I also knew that one day I would have to share everything with Uncle Keith and Alex, but it wouldn't be anytime soon.

CHAPTER 16

Finals and graduation were only a few months away. Being around Uncle Keith, Aunt Hope, and Alex had softened me a bit, but I was still unforgiving and had not dealt with any of the demons from my past. Going back home after graduation was not an option. I had promised myself that I would never live in the same house with daddy.

Now, I would need a job immediately after graduation, so I applied and received an internship at Baker Technologies here in Jefferson City. It was the age of the technology boom. CD players, cell phones, and desktop computers were all the rage, so there was a huge demand for computer analyst and programmers. So much so, I was asked if I could start working before I actually graduated. Thankfully, I was able to make arrangements with my instructors and start working immediately, the salary and benefits were excellent.

I met a man named Damon Carter who also worked at Baker on the same floor but in a different department.

He had been pursuing me since the first day I started. One particular day he sent an email and asked if he could take me to lunch. Reluctantly I agreed. He seemed nice, very intelligent and well spoken, unlike the knuckle heads I had been involved with in the past; he was polished and very successful.

Damon took me to a very nice restaurant not far from the office. Surprisingly, he didn't talk much about himself he wanted to know all about me. Of course, I was reserved and shared very little. Although he was pretty impressive, I was still cautious. There was no way I was going to let history repeat itself. On the way back to the office he asked if he could call me sometime. I agreed and gave him my number.

Damon and I spoke on the phone for several weeks before I agreed to go out with him again. When he picked me up from my dorm I thought he would wait outside, but he insisted on coming to my room to escort me back to the car. When he arrived I was in the bathroom adding the final touches to my makeup, so Iverem answered the door. I heard them chit-chatting a bit until I was ready. When I made my entrance he stood, "You look amazing Angel."

"Why thank you kind Sir."

"This one's a smooth one, you better watch out." Iverem commented.

Damon laughed and escorted me to the car. He was such a gentleman. He opened every door for me and held my hand as we walked. At dinner I asked him how old he was.

"I'm thirty. Is that too old for twenty-two year old?"

"How did you know I was twenty-two?"

"One of my responsibilities at Baker is to select new interns. I chose you. Not only do I know your age, but also your GPA, and every score on all your exams."

"Oh my, you've done your homework."

"I take my job seriously. Out of all the candidates, you were the best. You've worked hard for it so you deserve it."

"Well, thank you," I smiled.

"So Ms. Angel, what are your plans after you graduate?"

"I'd love to build my career with Baker Technologies. Who knows, maybe one day I'll be the CEO." I chuckled. "But, seriously, I want to be positioned financially to be able to put my brother, Alex, through college.

"That shouldn't be a problem," he replied.

Damon was wonderful. He shared his dreams and goals with me as we took long walks together. Our relationship grew sweeter as the days went by. It was everything I desired, but thought I would never have.

Finally, I decided it was time to introduce Damon to Uncle Keith, Aunt Hope, and Alex. Damon took us all to dinner at La' Madame's, a wonderful 4 star French restaurant. He was his normal charming self. Uncle Keith and Alex seemed to like him, but Aunt Hope was kinda quiet. I think she had her spiritual antennas up.

Damon even planned a surprise party for my

graduation. He helped me mail out my invitations then took me shopping and bought me the most beautiful dress and shoes for the ceremony. I couldn't wait to get home and show them to Iverem. "Ah, this one has very expensive taste. He loves throwing his money around."

"Damon just cares for me and that's his way of showing it. I didn't ask for any of this stuff. Actually, those swanky places are really not my cup of tea."

"Well, they are obviously his, so be careful or that smooth talk'n man will have you drinking from a different cup of tea," she said in her thick accent.

"Oh, Iverem, don't be such a skeptic. Damon's a great guy."

One Saturday, Damon and I went to lunch and afterwards he wanted to go to the Galleria Mall with all the pricy stores. I jokingly told him what Iverem said, but he was not amused at all. "Oh, Damon, she was just kidding around, you know her."

"I know her better than you do."

"What are you talking about; you've only known her for a few months."

"Well, I know she's your friend, so I didn't want to say anything, but…"

"But what, Damon?"

"She…she came on to me."

"What?! Not Iverem, you must have misunderstood."

"Angel, I came by your room and she answered the door and invited me in. She said you had run to check the mail and would be right back. So I came in and sat on your bed. She laid on her bed and raised her dress up pass her thighs so I could see her black lace panties. She told me she was an, *"International lover"* and once I had her, nobody else would be able to satisfy me. I asked her how could she do such a thing being your friend, but she just laughed and I walked out."

"What?! When did this happen? I can't believe she would do that to me!"

"You know how jealous some woman can be. She sees you have a good man and she has no one, so she goes after yours. I hate to say it, but it happens all the time."

"So that is why she's always making statements about being careful and watching you. She's the one I need to watch! I can't wait until I see her! I'm so sorry you had to go through that baby, but I'm so proud that you didn't yield to that witches temptation."

"Do you know how much I love you Angel? I would never hurt you. As a matter of fact, I've been thinking. How do you feel about us spending the rest of our lives together?"

"Damon, what are you saying?"

"Let's go back to my place." He looked at me with those gorgeous eyes and I melted.

"Let's go Baby." I spent the night. It was the first time Damon and I were intimate. I believed the intimacy was alright, after all, we were going to get married and spend the rest of our lives together.

"I can't wait to see that traitor!" I said when Damon dropped me off at my room.

"Go easy on her Angel, I don't blame her for being jealous of you, you're beautiful. You know she's just going to deny it ever happened, right?"

"Of course she will, but it doesn't matter. Our friendship is over!"

"You know I love you, right Angel?"

"Ah, yes and I love you too. How could I ever live without you?"

"You'll never have to worry about living without me Baby…ever." I had never heard such sweet words from any of the men I'd been with.

I sat waiting for him to come around to open my door like he usually did, but I guess he was just in a hurry. When I opened the door he blew me a kiss then drove off.

I stormed into my room. "Iverem, Iverem! Where are you?'

"For goodness sake, what are you screaming about, you'll wake the dead."

"How could you! What were you thinking? I bet you thought he wouldn't tell me."

"What in the world are you talking about?"

"I'm talking about you trying to seduce my man!!!"

"Where on earth did you get a crazy idea like that in your head?"

"Damon said you would deny it. You're such a liar!"

"Damon told you that? No, my dear, I'm afraid it's Damon that's the liar, not me. What kind of person do you think I am?!"

"I don't have to think anymore, I know! I cannot stand the sight of you, much less living with you. I'm moving out."

"Suit yourself. I knew that man was trouble the first time I laid my eyes on him."

"You will not talk about my man that way! He loves me and you can't stand it. You're green with envy!"

"Think what you want, but you don't have to move out, I'm moving out and I don't care if I ever see you again!" Iverem said as she slammed the door.

"Well, the feeling is mutual Honey!" I yelled.

Iverem slammed the door so hard the pictures fell off the wall. The next day when I got home, she and her things were gone. Damon had succeeded at removing the first special person from my life.

My graduation day was finally here. Damon had flowers delivered to my room early that morning. Uncle Keith, Aunt Hope, Alex and Sister Johnson were all there for my special day. I wanted to invite Aunt Joan, but I hadn't told anyone about her yet. She had asked me if I invited daddy, to which I answered, "Absolutely not!" He was the last person I wanted to see.

As I was standing back stage waiting for my name to be called to walk across the stage and receive my degree, I was thinking of Momma and how proud she would be. I had messed up big time, but I was back on track. I had a good man, even though I knew she wouldn't approve of me sleeping with him before we were married. All things considered, I think she would have been pleased.

"Ms. Angel Camille Sanders: Cum Laude."

"This is for you Momma," I said as I walked slowly across that stage.

Not wanting the moment to end, I could hear Uncle Keith, Alex, and even Aunt Hope yelling my name. I smiled as the Lexington University President handed me my degree and said, "Congratulations Angel, excellent job."

"Thank you Sir."

I did it!!! In spite of everything and everyone, I did it!!! We all celebrated at the dinner party Damon planned for me. He reserved a room at a beautiful Italian restaurant and the food was exquisite. Even Uncle Keith and Aunt Hope put their feelings about Damon aside that night. I felt so proud and accomplished as I sat next to him with his arms around me. It was a glorious, but bitter/sweet night because Momma wasn't there and Aunt Joan couldn't be there.

CHAPTER 17

D amon wanted me to move in with him after graduation, but I told him it would be disrespectful to my family. They were church going, God fearing people. He didn't like it, but accepted it. Instead, I found a cute little apartment off campus. Aunt Hope helped me pick out the furniture and decorate it. She had such great taste.

Everything had to be perfect before inviting Damon over to my new place for the first time. I prepared a romantic meal, chilled the wine and set the table with candles and a beautiful floral centerpiece. In the bedroom, rose pedals were sprinkled all over my bed and scented candles were strategically placed and all over the room. I took my time doing my hair and makeup. To top the night off, I wore a very cute little black dress. I wanted to be absolutely stunning for Damon.

The doorbell rang – he had finally arrived. I queued the music and opened the door. "Welcome to my humble abode, Mr. Carter."

"You look amazing, Baby."

"Thank you, honey, you look pretty amazing yourself. Come in and have a seat."

Damon sat down on the couch and crossed his legs. "Well, how do you like what I've done with the place, baby?"

"Where did you get this furniture?" He asked.

"Oh, Aunt Hope picked it out for me. Do you like it?"

"Well, not really. It looks pretty cheap," he said surveying the room and looking as if he smelled something foul.

"She thought it would be best for me to pay cash for everything, she didn't want me to get into a lot of debt and I agreed."

"If you ask me, you are too dependent on your family."

"It's not that Honey; we're just a close family. Speaking of family, you don't ever talk about your family," I said as I poured him a glass of wine.

"There's nothing to talk about. I've told you my mother and father are deceased and I'm an only child."

"No aunts, uncles or cousins?"

"Nope just me, I like it that way. I've seen families tear each other apart – no thanks," he committed as he took a sip of wine.

"My family isn't like that. Well, at least Uncle Keith, Aunt Hope, and Alex aren't."

"It's just that I want it to be me and you right now. Our relationship is growing and in order for us to get to know one another we have to spend time together. Your Aunt Hope has already come between us."

"I don't think so, Damon. What makes you think that?"

"Well, first of all, I wanted you to move in with me, but your precious family wouldn't approve. Then I wanted to buy the furniture for you, but your Aunt Hope stole that from me too. Nice furniture, not this cheap looking stuff. Can you understand what I'm saying, Baby."

"Yeah, well, I guess so. Come on, I know you're hungry. I've prepared a delicious meal for you."

I took his hand and escorted him to the table, put on my little black apron, prepared his plate and placed it in front of him then opened his napkin and placed it in his lap. I sat down bowed my head and waited. When I heard him pick up his fork I looked up. "Oh, I'm sorry; I thought you were going to say grace."

He shook his head and looked disgusted. "Look, I've had a long hard day, can we just eat?"

"Sure Honey."

He took his first bite of my homemade lasagna. I waited for some kind of expression or comment. "How do you like the lasagna?"

I waited in anticipation. "It's okay, I've had better."

"I'm sorry, it's usually really good." I was crushed after working so hard. I really wanted the evening to be special, but I was ruining it. "I have a surprise for you. I haven't even told my family, you're the first to know."

"Oh, God, you're not pregnant are you?"

"Uh, no, no Honey, it's nothing like that. I was offered a management position at Hendricks Technologies."

"You turned it down, right?"

"No Honey, I accepted it. It's much more lucrative and the benefits are amazing. More than that, the job I itself is exciting and challenging."

"Angel, you didn't even talk to me about it. You just took the job! I may have been able to get you more money at Baker. I could have helped with promotions, but you didn't give me the opportunity."

Damon was so aggravated, or maybe he was just disappointed. After all, he was responsible for getting me the internship at Baker. I understood why he may have felt I was being ungrateful.

I can see it so clearly now, this was the first of many excuses I would make for Damon, just like Momma did for daddy.

"This is what I'm talking about Angel. You don't consider or respect me at all."

"No Honey, that's not it. I really thought you would be excited for me."

"Well you thought wrong, Angel!" He got up from the table, drank the rest of his wine, slammed the glass into the fireplace and walked out.

Shocked, I ran after him. "Damon, Damon, please

come back inside. I'm so sorry. Honey, please come back. I'll call and tell them I changed my mind. Just don't leave like this. I'll try to do better, I promise. Come back inside, please. I just want to please you Baby."

Again, I used my body to barter. Sex for love, but it was just a placebo. He stopped, calmly took my hand and came back inside. I closed the door and turned to apologize again, the look he gave me chilled me to the bone. "You want me to stay, Baby?"

"Yes, yes, I do Honey. Please stay."

"Then beg."

"What? I don't know what you mean."

"I mean, get down on your knees and beg me. Do you know how many women would love to have a good man like me? If you want me...beg."

I couldn't believe what he was asking me to do. What trumps that is that I actually got on my knees and begged him not to leave me. Yet another means of control and manipulation. It was like teaching a dog obedience and submission by making it clear he was the dominant one and I would obey.

It was my own brokenness that allowed him to convince me that he was doing me a favor by lowering himself to be with someone like me. While my brokenness certainly was not my fault, it was my choice to remain broken. He was still pretty angry, but I knew it would all blow over once I satisfied him in my bed of rose petals. I had to make him realize how much I loved and respected him.

The next day I called Aunt Hope to get her take on

the situation. I wanted to know what she thought about me taking the job at Hendricks Technologies without consulting Damon first. "Angel, you're just dating Damon, he's not your husband; he's not even your fiancé. You made the choice to do what was best for you. I'm proud of you. You should stick to your decision and take the job."

I feared bringing the subject up to again. I was learning fast that Damon's mood could change without warning, so I decided to let sleeping dogs lie and called Hendricks Technology and declined their offer.

The next day I called Damon and told him I didn't take the job, he was pleased. "That's my girl. All I want to do is love you, provide for you, and protect you, Angel. Please, let me do that for you. You deserve it."

"I will Baby, thank you for loving me."

"Hey, let's celebrate. Just you, me and a bottle of Dom Perignon. What do you say Baby?"

"Absolutely! Can't wait to see you Damon.

CHAPTER 18

Baker had me leading a special project with several of our top computer analysts, most of which were men. Damon walked into my office while one of the younger analysts and I were deciding which company we should go with for the best production. "Oh, hey Damon, this is Charles Brighton; he's one of the analysts on the project."

"Pleased to meet you Damon," Charles extended his hand.

Damon ignored the gesture. "Angel, may I speak with you a moment."

"Sure, just give me a minute to wrap up with Charles. The boss wants a decision by noon today."

Damon excused himself without saying a word. I was a little embarrassed. "He seemed friendly," Charles chuckled.

"Yeah…right. Let's wrap this up shall we." I couldn't wait to talk to Damon about the way he embarrassed me, but I knew I had to do it very carefully. I didn't want him to think I was disrespecting him.

After Charles left I went to Damon's office and his secretary told me he had left for the day. I tried calling him several times, but no response. I wrapped up my day at the office and before heading home, decided to pick up dinner from one of my favorite spots. When I pulled up to my apartment, I spotted Damon sitting in his car. "Oh, he's here, good."

I was struggling to gather my things from the car and I thought he would've helped, but he just sat and watched. I fumbled for the key to unlock the door, walked in, sat my things down and waited for him to come in. I heard footsteps and assumed it was Damon, but to my surprise, it was Aunt Hope.

"Oh, hi Aunt Hope, come on in."

"Hey my Dear, how are you?"

"I'm good. I'm good – surprised to see you. Is everything okay?"

"Oh, yes. No need for alarm. Our Women's Ministry was thinking of holding its annual conference at the Peaceful Haven Resort about thirty minutes from here. Since I was already in your neck of the woods, I decided to stop by. And…I had to tell you face to face that Uncle Keith and I are pregnant!"

"How wonderful!!! You scared me for a minute. How many months are you? We've gotta think of a name. Is it a boy or a girl?"

"Slow down Angel," she laughed. "I'm only about

eight weeks, so we have a little time. If it's a girl, we want to name her Donna, after your mother."

Tears immediately welled up in my eyes. "Momma, would have loved that."

"No tears now, you're gonna make me start."

Just then I looked up and Damon was standing in the doorway. "Hi Damon, it's good to see you again. How have you been?" Aunt Hope asked as politely.

"Hi Hope, I'm doing well, thanks for asking. So, what are you two celebrating?"

"Aunt Hope and Uncle Keith are going to have a baby. Isn't that wonderful?"

"Well, congrats Hope. I guess the boyfriend is always the last to know."

"It's not like that Damon," she explained. "I just told Angel a few seconds ago."

"Sure...I'm happy for you both. As for me, I don't want any little crumb snatchers. You know the saying, right Hope?"

"No, I'm afraid I don't Damon. Please, enlighten me."

"Kids are great as long as they belong to someone else."

"Damon, stop teasing Aunt Hope. He's just kidding," I defended.

"I don't need you to speak for me Angel. I'm a grown man, I can handle myself. I simply don't like kids. Is that a crime?"

"Well, no, of course not Baby. I just didn't know you didn't want kids. We've never discussed it."

"Nothing to discuss." he said rudely.

"I guess I'm blessed to have a man that respects me enough to discuss these kinds of things with me," Aunt Hope fired back.

"Um, Aunt Hope, actually, that's why Damon is here. We kinda have some things to discuss. I really hate to rush you and thanks so much for delivering the good news in person. Please give Uncle Keith a big kiss for me."

I really felt bad for rushing her after she stopped by just to tell in person. I ushered her out the door and walked her to her car. "Angel, I don't like that man. He's disrespectful and obnoxious."

"You just have to get to know him Aunt Hope. He's really a great guy. He's under a lot of pressure at work and..."

Excuse number two.

"You really need to pray about going forward with this relationship Angel."

"It's okay Aunt Hope, it really is." She gave me a hug, got in her car and drove off.

I walked in the house and slammed the door. "How could you talk to my Aunt Hope like that?"

"How could you stand there and let her disrespect me like that?! She has never liked me and she doesn't even know me. She's the type of woman that wants to control and rule a man. Well she'll never control me!"

"Damon, that's not true. Aunt Hope..."

"So now you're calling me a liar? Look at you Angel! Defending her and not standing up for your man. Haven't I showed you I love you and want to take care of you? You have got to stop letting people come in between us. Like that dude in your office today. I saw how he was checking you out. And you, all grinning and cheesing in his face."

"What are you talking about Damon? I think you may be a bit jealous!"

When he walked towards me, I was familiar with the look in his eyes. I had seen it many times before. He grabbed my face with both hands, his manicured nails dug into my skin. "Don't you ever, ever, talk to me like that again," he said in a soft, deep voice before placing his hands around my neck. "Do you know how easy it would be right now for me to snap your little neck?"

"But I would never do that Angel, because I love you, but don't ever tempt me again. Now, be a good girl and say, "Yes, I understand."

"Yes, I understand," I repeated as tears rolled down my face.

Damon grabbed both of my arms very firmly and laid me on the couch. He kissed me hard and passionately then slapped me so hard my ears started ringing. He got up, looked down at me but said nothing as he turned and walked out the door. How foolish I was? Why couldn't I see? I guess when you starving, you'll eat anything.

Jan Davis

CHAPTER 19

I pressed the "up" elevator button, "Six please," I requested of the tall gentleman that stood waiting for his floor. I wasn't sure what to expect from Damon today. I made him so mad last night. I don't know why I keep messing up. *'Damon is a good man,'* I convinced myself.

I put the key in the door to my office and to my surprise there were six vases with three dozen roses in each. I couldn't stop smiling and called Aunt Hope to convince her that Damon really did love me. "Good morning Aunt Hope. Guess what happened when I opened the door to my office this morning?"

I tried to describe the beauty of each dozen; the fragrance, the color, and how he must have spent a fortune, but she didn't seem impressed. Maybe Damon is right – she just doesn't like him. After my failed attempt to sway her opinion of him, I went to his office and knocked on his door. "Come in."

"Hey Baby! Thank you so much. The roses are absolutely lovely."

"I handpicked each one especially for you. I'm sorry about last night, Baby. It's just that I love you so much, I don't ever want to lose you."

"Damon, no man has ever said those words to me and meant it. I love you too, and I'm sorry. You're right; I do let people come between us, but not anymore. From now on it's you and me."

"That's how it should be Angel. I want to take care of you, protect you and I'll never let anyone or anything come between us. You're my lady, Angel – nobody but you."

I'm so in love with this man. No man has ever loved me like this before. He is my world,' I thought as I floated out of his office.

When I got off work, I pulled up to the mailbox, grabbed the mail and headed to my apartment. I changed out of my work clothes, got comfortable on the couch and begin going through the mail, smiling as I opened the invitation from Alex. I couldn't believe he was graduating from high school already. Where had the time gone? He also included a picture of his prom date, what a cute couple.

Alex was so handsome, wearing a black tux with a midnight blue vest and bow tie. His date wore a strapless midnight blue gown with sequins and a short train. Immediately, I grabbed the phone and called him. "Hey Angel."

"Hey, lil' bro. I got the invitation to your graduation. You know I wouldn't miss it for the world."

"Yeah, it's cool. I'm just glad it's over and I'm finally done."

"Done? Boy, you're just getting started. What about college?"

"Yeah, well, I've been thinking a lot about that and I'm not sure if I want to do college."

"You don't want to do college?! Momma would have had a fit if she heard you say that. How are you going to get a good paying job and take care of yourself?"

"I'm thinking about joining the Air Force like Uncle Keith. He loves it, and he's seen the world."

"Have you talked to Uncle Keith about it?

"Actually, I have. We've talked quite a bit. I've even talked to the recruiter."

"You've never said anything to me about this Alex."

"I know Angel. I just didn't want you to freak out. I'm tired of this town and I need to learn to be my own man."

"Well, I can understand that. Daddy certainly hasn't been a shining example. I want you to follow your dreams Alex. I just don't want anything to happen to you. I don't know what I would do."

"I've thought about that too, but God has me. I'll be fine, so don't worry."

"Yeah, well, you know how I feel about God and how He feels about me."

"You've gotta let it go Angel. You've gotta forgive daddy – I have. It hasn't been easy, but with God's help I've forgiven him. Healing comes with forgiveness"

"Forgive him! Have you forgotten everything he did to us and Momma? I hate him for everything he did to me! Do you know he's been lying about having all those brothers? He had one brother, and he killed him."

"What?! What are you talking about Angel?"

I didn't want to tell him that way, but decided to tell him everything Aunt Joan told me. Alex was surprised of course, but I was surprised at the way he handled the news. He simply thanked me for telling me and said he understands daddy even better now. He even asked me for her phone number so he could introduce himself and invite her to his graduation.

For the life of me I just don't get that forgiveness stuff. I can't let daddy off that easy. I decided I might as well tell Uncle Keith too, so I called him. He basically had the same reaction as Alex. All was well, until he changed the subject to Damon. "Angel, you know I love you, but I gotta be honest. I really don't care for that Damon guy."

"Why? What did Aunt Hope tell you?"

"She didn't have to tell me anything, there's something about him that's just not right. I'm surprised you don't see it yourself."

"Uncle Keith, I love you too, but you just don't know Damon. He loves me and he treats me special. Do you know that today he sent me dozens, not one, not two, but dozens of roses? I was the envy of every woman at work. He's always telling me how special I am to him. You guys really haven't given him a chance."

"I tell you what, why don't you, Aunt Hope and Alex come to dinner next Sunday? "We can sit down and you all can really get a chance to know each other."

"Let me check with Hope, but I don't think it will be a problem. I'll do it for you."

"Thanks Uncle Keith. He's a great guy, you'll see." It was good to get all that stuff about daddy out in the open. I couldn't wait to tell Damon that Uncle Keith and Aunt Hope were extending the preverbal, *"olive branch"* and agreed to come to dinner and get to know him better.

As I headed for the shower the doorbell rang. Wondering who it could be, I detoured to answer it. "Hey Damon, I wasn't expecting you tonight." He was visibly agitated about something. "Thank you again for all the beautiful roses. I was the envy of every woman at the job today."

No response.

"Damon, what's the matter? Are you okay?"

"I'm fine Angel. Make me a key tomorrow; I'm tired of ringing the doorbell to my woman's house."

"Well, you don't look fine. I can see you're upset. Don't you want to talk about it? Maybe I can help."

"Stop hounding me, I said I'm fine! Now go get me something to drink."

"I'm not hounding you sweetheart. I see you're upset and I'm just concerned."

"Will you please, just shut up and get me a drink?"

"Yes, yes. All I have is wine, is that okay?"

"Yeah, just stop talking and get it."

I hurried to the kitchen, grabbed a glass and poured the wine. I hand it to him; and he quickly emptied it and hands it back for more. "Hey Baby, I've got some good news."

"I could use some good news right now. What is it?"

"I know you and my family haven't hit it off, but I explained to them what a wonderful man you are and they just haven't gotten the chance to really get to know you."

"And…"

"Well, I invited them to dinner next Sunday. I'm going to cook a wonderful meal and we're all going to sit down and talk so they can get to know and love you like I do."

"What?! There you go again! Did you ask me first? Did it ever enter into that empty head of yours to check with me? I might have plans."

"Damon, it's really not that serious. I'm sorry; I just wanted them to get to know you better."

"Why? So they can give me the 3rd degree? Your family is so controlling. It's time for you to cut the apron strings. You're a grown woman, but you have to consult with them about everything you do. You would rather please them than please me!"

"That's not true Damon," I explained placing my hand on top of his. "You know how I feel about you, but they are my family and I love them too. I know you don't have family, so it's harder for you to understand, but…"

Before I could finish my statement, he slapped me. "I warned you! Don't you ever, talk to me like that again! You will respect me!" He slapped me again. "It's time I teach you a thing or two about mouthing off and disrespecting me."

"Baby, no, I would never disrespect you. I respect you, I really do," I tried to explain.

Damon unbuckled his belt, and then slid it slowly out of the belt loops. "Damon, please. What are you doing? Oh, please don't!!!" He rolled the buckle end of the belt around his hand. I tried to run, but he grabbed me by my hair and threw me down onto the couch. He raised the belt in a rage and beat me. I begged him to stop. I apologized, anything to get him to stop, but nothing helped. He became even more enraged with each swing of his belt.

The sting and power of each lick was unbearable. I fell to the floor and tried to crawl out of reach, but he grabbed my leg and pulled me back. Then he threw the belt down and laid on top of me. I was crying and begging him to stop as I struggled to get free. He put both of his hands on each side of my face and kisses me. Then he began to cry, "I'm so sorry Angel. I'm so sorry. Why did you make me do this? Why! I love you so much Angel, I'm so sorry."

While he was crying and apologizing, I was thinking the same thing, *'Why do I continue to do this? Damon is a good man and look at what did I make him do.'*

149

"Angel, I'm so sorry. It will never happen again. Just don't leave me. I need you Baby, please, I'm so sorry. Why did you make me do this? I never wanted to do this."

"I know you didn't Baby. I'm sorry for aggravating you. I can't seem to do anything right. Please forgive me. Damon, I promise I will never disrespect you again. My family doesn't have to come to dinner. I'll tell Uncle Keith you have to work."

I later realized it was the brokenness I chose to hold onto that actually facilitated the abuse. Manipulation and control were twin terrors in his toolkit. My brokenness allowed him to master their use.

CHAPTER 20

The next morning I didn't know what to expect or what kind of mood he would be in. I wanted to make sure I said and did all the right things. I didn't want to disrespect him again…ever. I got up and quietly went into the bathroom to take a shower. The hot water stung the open wounds on my arms, back and legs. Tears streamed down my face and for the first time in a very long time the thoughts came back with a vengeance.

"Look at you! Beaten again. It's your life Angel, and this is always how it's going to be. It's all you deserve. You took a good man like Damon and look what you've turned him into. You'll never be happy; you'll never know real love because you don't deserve it. Do the world a favor, Angel…end it all. Alex is a grown man now, he can take care of himself."

I tried to combat the thoughts, but had no ammunition to fight. Defeated, I sank to the floor and agreed. Suddenly, Damon called my name and immediately I jumped up and answered before he came into the bathroom. "Good Morning. I'm in the shower Baby, can I get you something?" I said, carefully choosing my words.

"No Baby, I was just saying good morning to my favorite girl. Hey, let's call in sick today. I've got a surprise for you. Hurry and get dressed, I can't wait to show you!"

I was so relieved he was in a good mood. He was acting as if last night never happened. As I got dressed he suggested I wear long sleeves or a jacket and pants. "I don't want to see those whelps, they look awful," he said. I suppose he had totally forgotten he put them there. I still wondered what made him so upset last night.

Damon took me to breakfast and then we headed to the mall. When we arrived, he put a blindfold on me. He was as excited as a kid at Christmas. He held my hand as he led me into a store. When he took the blind fold off, there was a young man standing in front of me holding a black box with the most beautiful diamond ring I had ever seen.

I turned and looked at him as he went down on one knee. "Angel, I love you so much. I would be the happiest man on earth if you would agree to marry me."

I was so amazed; there were people clapping and cheering for us. The man who had beat me last night was on bended knee proposing to me the very next day. "Yes, yes! I'll marry you!"

Damon grabbed the ring out of the box and placed it on my finger. He even arranged for us to have a glass of champagne at the store. It was all so romantic; I convinced myself that what happened the night before would never happen again. I mean, look at what he just did. He actually wanted to marry me...me! I was so happy and excited.

"Damon, how...when did you plan all of this?"

"I looked at you sleeping Baby, you were so beautiful. I decided at that very moment that I wanted to spend the rest of my life with you. So, I made a few calls and there you have it."

On the way home, Damon was talking about how happy I had made him, while I was thinking about how I would tell Uncle Keith, Aunt Hope, and Alex about his proposal. I was admiring my beautiful engagement ring when I suddenly realized I had a wedding to plan. Damon looked at the panic on my face, "What's wrong Angel?"

"I...we have a wedding to plan! We need a date. Oh, and a beautiful venue. I love rich jewel tones, what do you think? Oh, and we need to put our heads together on the guest list. Who's gonna be your best man?"

"Hold on Baby, you're going 90 miles a minute, slow down!"

"It's just that there's so much to do."

"Yeah...I wanted to talk to you about that. I never wanted a big wedding. All the phony relatives and the expenses, it's just all so overrated. I was hoping I could just whisk you away to Hawaii and we could get married there."

"That's so sweet Honey, but every girl dreams of her

wedding day and when the time finally comes she wants it to be exactly the way she dreamed."

"Baby, don't make this an argument, it's supposed to be a happy time. You know your family doesn't like me and I don't want or need their opinions on this. Check your work schedule and see when you can take a week of vacation and we'll be on our way. I want you all to myself."

"Of course Honey, I guess. I'll just call Alex and the family and give them the good news."

"I told you, I don't want their opinion on this. You can give them the news after we're married." I wanted to disagree, but it wasn't worth setting him off again, so once again, I was compliant and said nothing.

Three weeks later, I found myself on a beautiful beach in Maui vowing to love, honor, obey, and cherish until death do we part. Exotic tropical flowers filled the lobby of the five star hotel. "Good Morning Sir and Ma'am. Welcome to the beautiful Flower of Maui Hotel. How may I assist you today?"

"Good morning, I am Mr. Damon Carter and this is my lovely soon-to-be bride, Angel Sanders. We have reservations for the week in your honeymoon suite."

"Yes Sir, I have your reservation right here," he said as he rang for the bell hop. "Please take Mr. Carter's bags to room 912."

"Yes Sir."

The bell hop gathered our bags and Damon tipped him for his service. "Mr. Carter and Ms. Sanders, welcome to our beautiful island. I have taken the liberty of placing a few amenities in your suite that I believe will be to your liking. The view from your balcony is quite breathtaking, do enjoy it."

"Here are your keys, Sir. Please take the elevator to your left up to the ninth floor and your suite will be to the right. Please let me know if I there is anything further with which I can assist. "

"Thank you, my man."

"You're quite welcome, Sir."

When we made our way to the elevator there was a lovely young lady who placed colorful, sweet smelling lei's around our necks. "Now that's what I call service, Baby. For the money I'm spending, I expect nothing less than the very best."

Damon put the key in the door, when he opened it the extravagance of the room took my breath away. The view of the crystal blue ocean set in a backdrop of majestic mountains was amazing. There was champagne chilling and chocolate covered strawberries on the glass dining room table. It really was paradise. Even in the midst of all the beauty, I was still heartbroken that my family wasn't there. I knew they would be very disappointed.

Our wedding ceremony was held on the beach at sunset. Brilliant shades of orange, pink, and purple colored the sky as the sun sank into the crystal blue water. Damon and I stood between two columns lit with white lights. The tops of each column were adorned with an amazing display of white tropical flowers accented with satin ribbon. It was simple but very elegant. I wore a fitted candlelit color gown. It draped softly on my shoulders before plunging in the back, and then fanned out at the bottom. I wore my hair down with one side pulled back behind my ear, adorned with an Amazon Lily.

Damon sported a black tux with a white shirt and white bowtie. We were both barefoot in the sand. "I now pronounce you husband and wife. Mr. Carter, you may kiss your bride." And with that, it was done. I was married. I was Mrs. Angel Camille Carter and I was terrified…what had I done? I tried to enjoy the rest of the trip, and Damon was a perfect gentleman the entire week, but I couldn't shake the bad feeling. Before I knew it, we were on a plane heading back home.

I told Uncle Keith and the family I was going to Hawaii with Damon, but I was ordered not to tell them we would be married there. I was so nervous my hands were trembling as I dialed Alex's number. "Hey lil' brother, how are you?"

"Hey Angel! Are you back from Hawaii?"

"Yes, Alex. We got back today and I have souvenirs for you all. Uhhh, I've got some wonderful news."

"Great, what's up?

"I guess I just need to say it. Damon and I got married in Hawaii."

"What?! Angel, you got married and didn't tell me? Does Uncle Keith and Aunt Hope know?"

"Uhhh, no, no they don't. I'm gonna call them next."

"Angel, you hardly even know this dude. Have you

even met his parents? Do they know you guys are married?"

"Damon is a very private man. He rarely talks about his family. He told me both his parents are deceased and he has no siblings, so there's really not much to talk about I guess."

"Do you at least know where he's from?"

"Alex, don't worry. He loves me and I love him, that's all that really matters."

"I hope you know what you're doing Angel, and I know Uncle Keith is going to be so disappointed when you tell him…I'm praying for you."

After hanging up with Alex, I called Uncle Keith, and Alex was right, I could hear the disappointment in his voice. I tried to soften the news by talking about the baby first, but it didn't help. I reassured him that everything would be fine and Damon was a really good man. He finally said I was a grown woman, and while he and Aunt Hope didn't agree with my decision, they would respect it. He asked me if I had told daddy, but I changed the subject.

Uncle Keith told me they were going to throw Alex a surprise party right after his graduation. "What a great idea, Alex deserves it."

"I met a few of his friends at the game, so I'll invite them," he said in a not so chipper voice.

"Uncle Keith, is there anything I can do to help with the planning?"

"I'll let you talk to Hope, so you can ask her." She was just as disappointed as he was, but told me she would love my help with the food and decorations. We talked for about an hour finalizing the plans for the party and discussing names for the baby. Before we hung up, she told me she's always praying for me and she and Uncle Keith would always be there for me, no matter what.

Damon and I took off one more day to handle all of the necessary business. We went to the Social Security Office, the DMV and finally the bank. The next job to tackle was moving. I would be moving into Damon's house. Of course, he insisted I sell all my furniture. He said it just wasn't his taste.

I was hesitant to tell him about Alex's surprise graduation party. I never knew how he was going to react. That being the case, I decided to tell him in a public place just in case he got angry. After we moved the last box we stopped for a bite to eat. "A table for two please," Damon instructed the waitress.

"Hey Honey, I told my family we got married."

"I know that went over like a lead balloon," Damon said sarcastically as the waitress handed him the menu.

"No, sweetheart, they were happy for us. They were just disappointed they couldn't be there, that's all. Ummm, do you remember me telling you that Alex is graduating next month?"

"Yeah, what about it?"

The waitress took our orders and I continued, "Well, Uncle Keith and Aunt Hope are throwing him a surprise graduation party. I can't believe he's graduating already."

"That's nice, when is it?"

I was shocked at his calm response. "It's Saturday, the 25th. Aunt Hope asked me to help with the food and decorations. She's four months pregnant and I don't want her to overdo it. She could really use the help... is...is that okay with you?" I meekly asked as our drinks were placed on the table.

"I guess that's cool," he picked up his glass of wine and took a few sips.

"Great! Thanks Baby, I appreciate it. Springfield is a three hour trip from Jefferson City, so I figured we can leave that Friday night so I can be there to help with everything?" I said choosing my words wisely as our food was placed on the table.

"You can leave Friday. I never said I was going."

"Oh, but Damon, I don't want to go without you. It will be our first function together as husband and wife."

"Let's get something straight Angel. I don't like your family and they don't like me. I don't need their approval for anything I say or do, I'm a grown man. They are your family, not mine, so don't push it. Just be happy I'm allowing you to go. End of conversation."

Damon kept his composure, but his voice was very firm and his eyes dared me to challenge him. I didn't want things to escalate and him cause a scene, so I didn't say another word. I no longer had an appetite, so I quietly picked over my food as I tried to think of yet another excuse for him.

CHAPTER 21

As I made the three hour trip home, I rehearsed my excuse for Damon. When I pulled into the driveway of Uncle Keith and Aunt Hope's house, he met me outside. "Hey Mr. and Mrs. – Angel, where's Damon?"

"He's sorry he couldn't make it. He was called in on a major project at work at the last minute. He was so upset. It's the demands of being in executive management."

"We were so looking forward to seeing him, but, ya gotta do what'chu gotta do," Uncle Keith said empathically.

Aunt Hope came to the door and asked the same question. She was starting to show just a little and had such a beautiful glow. I told her the same lie, but I don't believe she bought it. She just smiled and looked at me. She always saw right through me.

I called Damon when I got settled, but got no answer. Aunt Hope and I got busy in the kitchen while

Uncle Keith tinkered with the decorations as best he could. We were so excited and having such a good time. I didn't realize how much I missed them. My only concern was seeing daddy. We hadn't seen each other since Uncle Keith's wedding.

We arrived at the graduation pretty early to make sure we got good seats. We made sure our cameras were ready and Uncle Keith was queuing up the camcorder when I felt a gentle touch on my shoulder. To my surprise, it was Aunt Joan. I was so happy to see her. I'm not sure why, but I was. I formally introduced her to Uncle Keith and Aunt Hope. They were so very gracious to her and invited her to sit with us. "Is John here too?" Aunt Joan inquired.

I looked at Uncle Keith for an answer as well. "Oh, he's probably running late. I called and left a message to let him know where we were sitting."

"Mr. Alex David Sanders: graduating with honors." The Principal announced. Alex was so handsome, as he walked across the stage with his head held high. I was so very proud of my brother. Daddy came to the graduation, but didn't sit with us, which was a wonderful thing in my opinion.

We left right after the ceremony to make sure we arrived at the venue before Alex and his friends. Aunt Joan was excited to finally meet him. She also wanted to talk to daddy again, but I still refused to forgive him. I hated the very air he breathed.

Alex's friends told him they were going to another one of their classmate's graduation party, he had no idea it was really his party. We all gathered around the entrance and anxiously waited for him and his entourage to arrive. The door slowly opened and he stepped in. "SURPRISE!!!"We almost scared him to death. He was really surprised.

Daddy didn't stay long and refused to speak to Aunt Joan and I refused to even make eye contact with him. After he left I enjoyed the remainder of the evening with my family. Aunt Joan, however, was disappointed in his departure.

I headed back home right after the party. I wanted to avoid the whole Sunday morning church thing. As I drove I wondered what I was driving back to. I made it home a little after 1 a.m. and thank goodness Damon was already asleep. I didn't want to wake him, so I went into one of the spare bedrooms. I turned on the light and quietly placed my bags on the bed. As I sat down to take off my shoes, I noticed a red folder sticking out from under the bed. Kneeling down beside the bed, I pulled out the folder and saw an old brown pair of boots with an odd imprint of a large cobra on the bottom of them.

Normally, boots under a bed wouldn't be an unusual thing, but Damon vehemently insisted that all of our footwear be in the closet neatly stacked in their original boxes. It was one of his many pet peeves. What a hypocrite. If he found a pair of my shoes under the bed it would be World War III and they were muddy too. But, what interested me most was what was in the folder.

I tipped back to our bedroom to make sure Damon was still sleeping; he was. I took the folder into the upstairs bathroom and locked the door. Inside the folder was mail – his mail. I looked at the letter on top and the return address was The Attorney General, Child Support Division. Now, why in the world would Damon be receiving mail from the Attorney General's Office? It was opened so I knew he had read the letter and it was dated three months ago, it read:

Damon Carter,

You are hereby placed on notice. Elizabeth Hicks has requested a hearing for child support determination on behalf of Heather Carter. You are hereby ordered to appear at the 127th District Civil Court on June 12th at 8:00 a.m.

"What?! Damon has a child? But he said he didn't want children. Heck, he didn't even like children. This is crazy. What else don't I know about this man? Who is he? Who did I marry?" I lay awake the rest of the night trying to figure out a way to ask him about the letter without him knowing I went through his things. I came up with a plan and hoped it would work. I couldn't take another beating.

Monday, I went to Damon's office and told him I wasn't feeling well and left work early. When he got home a few hours later, I lied and told him he had gotten a phone call from the Attorney General's Office of Child Support to remind him of his court date for a hearing concerning his daughter, Heather Carter. He just looked at me and walked out of the room. "Damon, please talk to me. What is this about? Do you have a daughter?"

"Well, now you know. So what are you going to do, leave me? Are you going to leave me Angel?!"

"No, no Honey, of course not. I'm your wife; I just want to know if you have a child and if so, why didn't you tell me about her?"

"Yes, I have a child!!!" He snapped. "Her mother deceived me and got pregnant on purpose. I didn't tell you because it wasn't your business then, and it's not your business now!"

"Damon, it's natural for me to have questions. How old is she? Do you get to see her? Do you even want to see her?'

"I'm not going to tell you again, Angel. Drop it!!!" Like the obedient wife I was trained to be, I didn't say another word, but my mind was going a hundred miles a minute. One thing was for sure, I was going to be in the 127th District Court on the 12th of June. For the next two weeks leading up to the court date, I tried to find more information. I wanted to see a Birth Certificate and locate her mother, Elizabeth Hicks, but was unsuccessful.

It seemed like it had been months, but the court date finally arrived. Damon never mentioned another word about Heather, her mother, or the court date. I had to be in that court room, but I definitely couldn't let Damon know I was there.

On the day of the hearing I went to work as usual, but left early to get there before Damon got there. Of course he didn't go to work. To execute my plan I bought a wig, glasses, and then dressed in some frumpy clothes so he wouldn't notice me. I camped out on a bench down the hall from the court room and waited for him.

Damon stepped off the elevator promptly at 8:45 and headed to the court room. He was so focused he never looked my way. I walked to the court room and peeped though the door to see where he was sitting. There he was, seated on the second row, left of the bench. I entered quietly and sat on the last row on the same side. While we waited for the judge to enter the court room I hid behind a book I pretended to be reading.

Damon was obviously agitated. I remembered the date on the letter and understood why he had come home agitated. It was the same day he beat the crap out of me with his belt. I wondered which one of the many women in court room was Elizabeth. I tried to watch his expressions for clues as he looked back at the doors whenever someone entered.

"Elizabeth Hicks vs. Damon Carter," the court clerk finally called. Elizabeth was a beautiful, very thin, white woman. She was professionally dressed in a navy blue suite with matching pumps. Her dishpan blond hair was carefully pulled back into a neat bun. It was interesting that even though she was in court, she made sure she kept her distance from Damon. There was a distinctive fear in her eyes. Instantly, I knew he had beaten her too.

Two attorneys approached the judge's bench. One of which was Damon's. *'This man has a lot of secrets,'* I thought as the scene played out before me. The attorneys spoke to the Judge and then to each other, but I couldn't make out what they were saying.

Damon looked at Elizabeth with the same look he gave me each time he hit me. She turned her face away quickly to avoid eye contact. It seemed that *"the look,"* still struck a chord of fear in her just as it did me. I thought I would have felt animosity towards her, but instead, I felt a strange sense of kinship.

The attorney's conferred with their clients a few minutes, then resumed their conversation with the Judge. After about thirty minutes the Judge picked up her gavel;

"Child Support is hereby awarded in the amount of $2,500.00 monthly, plus an additional $200.00 monthly for arrears, effective immediately, so ordered. Clerk, please prepare a writ to have all support withdrawn from Mr. Carter's payroll checks."

I jumped at the sound of her gavel striking the sounding block. *'Good for her,'* I thought. As they turned to walk away, I saw him say something to Elizabeth, but couldn't hear what he said. Whatever he said she was so visibly shaken by it that she cut the corner of the attorney's bench too short and tripped over the leg of the chair. Damon smirked as she tumbled to the floor and kept walking. I quickly put the book up to my face as he walked out of the courtroom, angry and cursing at his attorney.

Several people rushed to Elizabeth's aid. She was nervous and embarrassed but okay. She spoke with her attorney a few minutes before heading out of the court room. I followed her out and checked the long hallway for any sign of Damon before calling her name, "Elizabeth, may I speak with you for just a minute, please?"

Quite naturally she was guarded as I approached her. I smiled to try to ease her concern. "Hello, my name is Angel. I'm…I'm Damon's wife." She immediately turned and walked away. "Please Elizabeth; I'm not angry with you. He never told me he had a daughter. I just want to ask you a few questions." She picked up her pace, her heels clicking down the long hallway on the wooden floor. "He beat me too," I called out.

Several people stared, but I didn't care. She stopped and turned around with a look of sympathy on her face. I knew it was for me. I walked to her and extended my hand.

"Let's talk," she said softly. We walked together and sat on the same bench I'd sat on waiting for Damon to arrive. "How long have you been married?"

"Just four months. Were you married to him?"

"No, we lived together for four years – four horrible years. He wined and dined me at first. He was so charming I thought I had finally found the love of my life. I was terribly mistaken." She looked directly into my eyes and said, "You are too, Angel."

"Please, tell me everything Elizabeth. What happened between the two of you? He won't tell me anything."

"I'm so sorry." She held my hand and looked away as she told her story. "When I met Damon, he was focused on climbing the corporate ladder. My godfather was the Vice President of Baker Technologies at the time. He thought Damon was Baker's next brilliant young executive and was determined to help him get there. He carefully planned Damon's promotions from department to department."

"God rest his soul, he died before he got to know the *"real,"* Damon. Falling in love with him was easy. He was so kind and consoling when my godfather died. I got pregnant several months after I moved in with him. I really thought he loved me and we would get married and be a family, I was so naive."

"Damon never knew his father, and his mother was a drug addict. She abandoned him in a crack house and the state took custody. He ended up in foster home after foster home. Some were good, but far more were horrible. He was constantly beaten and sometimes starved for days at a time. Damon once told me one of his foster mothers would lock him in a closet for hours on end. He has two sisters and a brother, but he has no idea where they are. He was so young when they were separated he doesn't even remember how they looked." My heart broke for Damon as she unveiled his tragic story.

Elizabeth continued. "Damon was so angry when I told him I was pregnant. Well, he was angry period. He said I was trying to trap him to make him marry me. That's when the beatings began. I almost lost Heather several times. He told me he would kill me if I ever told anyone or I tried to leave him. I've had broken ribs, fingers and a broken jaw. He even pulled several plugs of my hair out once. The final straw was when he came home drunk one night. He beat me, and then raped me repeatedly."

"That night, I looked into the eyes of my frightened baby girl and somehow found the strength to leave him. I'm an only child; both my mother and father are deceased. Mother was an only child and my father's only brother preceded him in death and had no children. So I was all alone, just me and Heather. It was her love that kept me alive. There were so many days I simply would have ended it all if it wasn't for Heather. God knows just what we need. She was just a year old when we left."

Elizabeth reached in her purse and handed me a tissue as I wept. "I checked into a battered women's shelter called New Life. I finally got counseling, gave my heart to Jesus, and now I'm working on my degree. It certainly hasn't been easy, but God has helped me to rebuild my life."

"It's so strange though...after all this time, I still fear him. I thought I was passed all of that. Today was the first time I've seen him since I left. I'd never planned on seeing him again, but the State required me to file for child support in order to get assistance. I had no choice. Well, that's the whole ugly story."

"Do you have a picture of Heather?"

"Sure," she pulled her wallet from her purse. "This is a recent picture. She took it this year on Easter Sunday. She's three years old now. She'll be four next month. She's so smart and asks a million questions."

Heather had Damon's eyes and smile and Elizabeth's nose. Her hair looked like locks of spun silk and her skin was smooth and fair. "Oh Elizabeth, she's beautiful! You must be so very proud of her."

"Oh, I am. Jesus and Heather are the loves of my life."

"Damon is a very angry man, but he really does love me, Elizabeth. I'm going to help him get better. Would you mind if we exchange cell phone numbers?"

"That would be nice, but please, don't use my real name in your address book."

"Good idea, he would be livid if he knew I was even here today. Elizabeth, I saw Damon say something to you after the Judges verdict. May I ask what he said?"

"He threatened me. He said he would get me for this."

"He's just angry. He'll get over it, don't be afraid."

"Angel, I've worked so hard to get my life back. I refuse to give him power over me again. I'm not scared, I'll be just fine," she smiled.

"I've even taken a week of vacation, so maybe now that this is all behind us, Heather and I can spend some fun quality time together. She's been asking me to take her to the zoo. She absolutely loves the monkeys."

"That's great. A week to relax and enjoy that beautiful little girl of yours I believe is just what the doctor ordered. I'm so sorry for all you've gone through Elizabeth."

"Angel, you said he beat you too. The beatings will only get worse. I know you're hoping he will change, but a dark heart can only receive light through the power of God. Please, please, Angel, I beg of you…don't stay too long…"

CHAPTER 22

For some reason I figured, since I knew his story I could somehow fix him. Now, I know I can't fix anybody, nor can you help anybody that doesn't want to be helped. You can't want deliverance for someone more than they want it for themselves.

I knew Damon would be in a horrible mood and being at home alone with him would be treacherous, but there was no possible excuse could I use to stay out all night. I was startled when my cell phone rang. "Hello… Oh, hi Uncle Keith. How are you doing, is Aunt Hope okay?"

"Hi Angel, yeah, Hope and Alex are fine. Listen, where are you?"

"Oh, umm, I'm heading home. What's up? What's going on?"

"I need you to pull over, Angel."

"Pull over? Why?"

"Angel, listen, just do it. Please, pull over."

"Okay, okay. Just give me a minute." I pulled into a gas station, my heart was pounding. "Now, please tell me what's going on."

"Angel, it's your Dad. He had a massive stroke. He, he didn't make it Angel. He's gone."

"Where's Alex?"

"Don't worry, he's here with us. But he's taking it pretty hard."

"I'm on my way." I hated to admit it, but I actually thought, *Well daddy, you finally did something good for me. You died at the perfect time. Now, I have a great excuse not to go home tonight.*

I called Damon to give him the news and just like I thought; he was in a bad mood. "Where the hell are you, Angel?"

"Damon, it's my dad, he just died. He had a stroke. I'm on my way to Uncle Keith and Aunt Hope's house. Alex is there with them."

"Do you have to go now? I want you in my bed tonight."

"Damon, Alex is not taking it well. I really need to go home, you can understand that, right Baby? I'll call you as soon as I get there." He didn't respond, just hung up. I didn't have time to focus on Damon, I was worried about Alex.

Everything daddy did to me and Momma played in my head. All the abuse, the terrible things he said, the lies he told, even about his family. Just then I remembered Aunt Joan. She would be crushed. I hated to call her with the news, but I wasn't sure how she would know if I didn't tell her. "Hello."

"Hi Aunt Joan, its Angel."

"Well isn't this a pleasant surprise! It's so good to hear your voice my Dear."

"Are you at home? Can you talk for a minute?"

"I'm at work right now, but I can take a break. Let me wrap up my paperwork for this patient and I'll give you a call back in, say...fifteen minutes."

"Okay, that's fine; I'll speak with you then."

I called Sister Johnson, but got her voicemail, so I left her a message. What a crazy day it had been. My thoughts were racing once again. Damon has a daughter, which means I'm a step-mother, and daddy is dead. I tried to organize my thoughts to no avail. It was just too much. So I chose not to think at all and turned the radio up as I drove.

My phone rang, it was Aunt Joan. When I told her the news, she didn't say anything for several seconds. "Aunt Joan, are you okay?"

"I'm, I'm so... I just don't know what to say. I have prayed and prayed for him for so long...I just don't understand. But I know God is sovereign. His ways are not our ways, but they're always perfect. May I help with the plans?"

"Aunt Joan, we welcome your help. We welcome you into our lives. You're family."

"Thank you Angel. Thank you so much. You can't possibly know how much that means to me."

"I'll be spending the night at Uncle Keith's. Now that daddy's gone, I just realized I don't really know a lot about you."

"I guess you don't. We haven't really had a chance to talk again since the wedding. Well, I moved to Springfield right after I found John and shortly before Donna passed. I live about seven miles from your dad's house. I'm a registered nurse and I work in the ER at City General Hospital."

"City General, that's where they took Momma."

"Yes, I know Dear, I was part of Dr. Keller's team that tried to revive her. I didn't even know who she was until I saw John. It had been years since I'd seen her."

"Was she alive when she arrived? Did she suffer?"

"No, no she wasn't, we tried to resuscitate her for an hour. Just know she didn't suffer at all. As a matter of fact, I was amazed at how peaceful she was. I knew she had to have known the Lord."

"Yep, she made sure we were in church every Sunday."

After our conversation, I gave her Uncle Keith's address. "Alright, Honey I'll see you guys in the morning."

"Thanks, Aunt Joan, I'm looking forward to seeing you again."

I made it to Uncle Keith's house in two hours and ten minutes flat. I flung open the car door and was in a full sprint up the steps before I realized Alex was sitting on the porch. I ran to him and held him. "Angel, I'm so sorry. I feel like I am betraying you and Momma because

I loved dad. I know how much you hated him, I'm so sorry."

"Oh, no, no Alex. He was our daddy, he was good to you and he loved you. I'm sorry for putting you in the position to make to feel this way. It's okay to grieve Alex. It's okay to be sad. It's okay to hurt. I love you and I'm here for you."

Uncle Keith and Aunt Hope came to the door, but didn't disturb us. I was trying to think of a funny story about daddy, but there was nothing funny or happy about our life with him. But I did remember funny stories about me and Alex and in no time we were laughing. We all talked and laughed until we couldn't keep our eyes open. I was emotionally drained, but kept my promise and call Damon before I went to bed. "What took you so long to call me? Where are you?"

"I'm at Uncle Keith's house. I wanted to make sure Alex was okay."

"There you go again...what about me?"

"How did things go today in court?"

"What did you say?!"

"I said...how did things go in court today?" I was too tired to be afraid. There was no room on my emotional plate for fear.

"I'm going to ignore that comment since your dad died, but I'm not going to forget it."

I guess there was room for fear after all. I recanted and changed the subject. "Are you coming to the funeral Damon?"

"You couldn't stand him, so what's the big deal?"

"He's was still my father, Damon."

"I'm not a heartless man Angel, just let me know when and where."

"Thank you, I appreciate that Damon."

"By the way, I have to fly to New York in a week or so for business to meet with the directors for the Skylar Project."

"Oh, yeah. I heard about that. It's supposed to be a pretty big deal. But I thought it wasn't supposed to start until late next month?"

"Angel, what's with the third degree?"

"I'm sorry Damon. I guess I'm just really tired." We talked for a few more minutes, I took a quick shower and as soon as my head hit the pillow, I was out like a light.

My ringing phone broke my sleep. "Hello."

"Hi Precious, it's Sister Johnson. Did I wake you Darl'n?"

"Oh no, it's fine. How are you?

"How are you and Alex?"

"I'm fine, Alex took it pretty hard, but he's better now. The hard part will be when he has to go home and sort through daddy's stuff."

"Well, don't you worry Honey; I'm taking the first flight out in the morning."

"It will be so good to see you Sister Johnson."

"Let me know if there is anything I can do in the meantime."

"Yes Ma'am."

Damon actually showed up for daddy's funeral, but left immediately afterwards. He had that trip to New York on Monday, but mostly because he didn't want to deal with my family and I'm sure the feeling was mutual. I stayed another day to help go through daddy's things and get the finances in order.

Momma had taken out a $150k insurance policy on daddy years ago. I told Alex he could have it all. I didn't want a dime. We decided to pay off the mortgage and put the rest in the bank for Alex to use at his discretion.

Alex joined the Air Force and would be leaving for boot camp in ninety days. I thought the timing couldn't be better. I tried to convince him to stay with Uncle Keith, but he told me he would be fine, he was a grown man and wanted to stay home until he left.

It was time for me to get back home. I hadn't spoken to Damon in couple of days. I called him but he didn't answer. I left voice messages so he would know I wasn't disrespecting him. There was little time to think about our situation...until now.

CHAPTER 23

I was so glad I had another day off work and even more so that Damon had left for New York before I got home. I needed time to think and collect myself and assess my life. I especially needed to think about my conversation with Elizabeth, but first I just needed to relax.

As soon as I got home, I took a long bubble bath and drank a glass of wine to try to unwind but it didn't help much. Although it was 11:30am, I put on my robe and curled up on the couch with the remote – anything to take my mind off the drama of my life.

I was just about to call Damon again when the doorbell rang. I wondered who it could be, since I wasn't expecting anyone. "Who is it?"

"Delivery for a Mrs. Angel Carter."

I looked out the peep-hole then opened the door. "Sign here, please ma'am."

"They're lovely, thank you."

"You're welcome ma'am, have a good day." It was a beautiful bouquet of white tropical flowers, just like the ones at our wedding. What a surprise. Damon had been in such a foul mood lately I certainly wasn't expecting him to send me flowers. I couldn't wait to call him. "Aw, thank you so much. They're beautiful! What's the occasion?"

"I need to apologize to you, baby. Things have been crazy for me lately."

"You mean, the child support thing?" I was thinking it, but I couldn't believe I actually said it out loud.

"Yeah, yeah...but it's all over now. I took a paternity test and they read the results when I went to court. I'm not the father, so the judge threw the whole thing out. Can you believe that crazy woman took me through all of that for nothing? She actually had me thinking that kid was mine."

I listened as he lied to me, and so convincingly. I realized then, *'this man is a compulsive liar.'* If I hadn't been in the courtroom myself that day, I would have believed every word. What can he possibly be thinking?

"So it's all over and the child isn't yours. You don't have to pay child support?"

"That witch was nothing but a gold digger. I told her I never wanted children. She was just after my money, but she'll never get a dime now!"

I wondered if I had missed something in court that day. I had to call Elizabeth. Maybe something had happened since the court date. "Well, I can't wait to get home tomorrow. Hello, Angel?"

"Oh, I'm sorry…yes; I can't wait to see you either. You're only staying one day?" I asked with a hesitation in my voice.

"You sound disappointed."

"No, you know that's not true. I just thought you would be gone a little longer, but I'm so glad you coming home to me," I tried to sound convincing.

Immediately after Damon hung up, I called Elizabeth. One ring – two rings – three rings. "Oh pick up, please, Elizabeth, pick up…." Four rings.

"Hi, you've reached Elizabeth and Heather. We're not available, but please leave a message and we'll call you back. Bye."

"Umm, hi Elizabeth, this is Angel…Damon's wife. I hope you and little Heather having fun. Listen, Damon told me he took a paternity test and he's not the father, so the judge dismissed the case. Did I miss something? Is that true? Please call me back as soon as you can. Thanks…bye."

As soon as I hung up, my phone rang. I looked at the name, "Karen Woods." That's the alias I used for Elizabeth in my contacts. "Oh, hi Elizabeth, I'm so glad you called me back."

"Hello, this is Officer Earl Hammond with the Jefferson County Police Department. With whom am I speaking please?"

"Officer Earl Hammond? I'm sorry; I must have the wrong number."

"No ma'am. This is Elizabeth Hicks cell phone. Are you related to her?"

"No...yes...My husband is her daughter's father. Why do you have her phone? Where is she?"

"Ma'am, I'm so sorry, but she and her daughter have been in an accident."

"Accident?! What kind accident? Are they okay?"

My heart was pounding.

"Where are you ma'am? Is there a way you can come to the Police Station or I can come to you?"

"Please, what's happened?!"

"Ma'am, Elizabeth was killed in a car accident two days ago, but her daughter survived. She's in critical condition, but she's alive. We have been trying to locate her next of kin, but there were no names listed in her cell phone. The address on her driver's license isn't correct, so we haven't had much to go on. You're the first person that's called."

I couldn't talk. I couldn't breathe. "Ma'am, you still there?"

"Yes, yes. I'm here. Umm, Heather...what's the name of the hospital?"

"Ma'am, if you come into the station, I can give you more details."

"Yes, right...okay. I'll be there in thirty minutes." I just sat there and cried. I didn't even really know her, but somehow I felt connected to her.

When I arrived at the station, I asked for Chief Hammond at the front desk. "Yes, Ma'am, he's expecting you," the lady directed me to his office.

"Hello, Ma'am. I'm so sorry I had to give you the news over the phone. Are you okay?"

"Yes, I'm okay. I just don't understand what happened."

"She lost control of her car and veered into oncoming traffic on I44. It's a miracle the baby survived. Do you have some ID Ma'am?"

"Oh, yes. I'm sorry." I fumbled through my purse nervously for my wallet. "Here you go."

"Thank you Ma'am. Umm, may I ask, where your husband is?"

"Oh, he's out of town…on business. He's been away a couple of days."

"Well, I hate you have to break the news to him. It's so sad. Did she have any other relatives?"

"No Sir. Her parents are deceased and she has no siblings. She came from a very small family. Where… where have they taken her?"

"Her remains are still at the County Hospital, in the morgue. Are you able to take care of her final arrangements?"

"Yes…yes Sir, I guess we'll have to."

"Please fill out this form, so I can release her personal items to you and we will notify you when our investigation is complete."

"Investigation? I thought you said it was an accident."

"Every accident that results in a fatality is investigated. It's just routine Mrs. Carter."

"I understand. Thank you." I completed the form. A few minutes later he came back and gently placed a yellow envelop on his desk in front of me. Instantly, I burst in to tears. "This is...this is her life, in this little yellow envelop?" I don't know if I was crying for her or the "*her*," in me.

After I composed myself, Chief Hammond walked me to the door. How in the world would I handle this with Damon? I didn't have time to think about it, I headed to the hospital to be with Heather. I hated to think she had been alone there for two days.

Frantically, I ran into the hospital to the Patient Information desk. "Hello, my name is Angel Carter. I'm here to see Heather Carter please."

"Are you related?" The nice lady inquired.

"I'm her...her step-mother." The words sounded foreign as I spoke them. '*Me, a mother.*'

"May I see your ID please?" I handed her my driver's license. She looked at my license and back at me again. "Thank you Ma'am," she handed it back. I was in such a hurry and it seemed she was moving in slow motion. "She's in room 425. Here's a visitors name tag for you. Now, if you go down this hall you'll see a set of elevators on your right. Just take those up to the 4th floor. Room 425 is to your left."

"Thanks," I grabbed the name tag and rushed to the elevators. On the way up, I wondered what I would say to her. She had never seen me and I'm sure all she wants is her mother. I knew exactly how that felt.

The doors open and I make my way to her room. "Good evening Ma'am. Who are you here to see today?"

"Heather…Heather Carter in room 425."

"May I see your ID please?"

I was still holding it in my hand. "Thank you Ms. Carter. Are you related?"

"Yes, I'm her step-mother."

"I'm so glad to see you! I was so worried for that precious little girl. I'll escort you to her room."

It was more like a ward. There was a nurse's station surrounded by rooms with a team of nurses carefully keeping watch. I followed the nurse to 425. "Here she is. She's just beautiful? Do want me to wake her?"

"No, please. Let her rest. How is she doing?"

"She was critical, but the doctor just upgraded her to stable, but serious. She's a fighter I tell you. It's a miracle she's alive. Not only that, but she has no broken bones or lacerations. She did have some blood in her urine. We ordered an MRI the first set showed a small puncture in her liver. The doctor ordered another one today, and there's no trace of it now. Yep, it's certainly a miracle."

"Thank you Ma'am. Thank you all for taking such good care of her."

"Don't thank us, thank God. It's a miracle I tell you," she declared again as she walked out.

I moved closer to her bed. She was beautiful. Her picture didn't do her justice. I gently touched her arm and she opened her eyes, looked at me, smiled and sweetly said, "Can you find my mommy? She's lost."

My heart broke. "Hi Heather, my name is Mrs. Angel. How are you feeling?"

"I want my Mommy," she began to cry.

I didn't know what to say or what to do. Then I remembered Momma singing to me, so I sang to her. *"Yes Jesus loves you. Yes Jesus loves you. Yes Jesus loves you, for the Bible tells you so."* She stopped crying and to my surprise, began to sing with me until she slowly drifted back to sleep. When she closed her eyes I kissed her forehead.

One of the nurses came into the room to check her IV. "What's going to happen to her?"

"I'm so sorry for your loss. I'll give you the name and number of the Social Worker assigned to her. Give her a call tomorrow and she'll explain everything to you."

"Thank you so much." I gave Heather another kiss goodnight, followed the nurse to her station and got the information before leaving the hospital.

Again, all I could think about was how much of a whirlwind my life had been the last few months. I got married, daddy died, Alex joined the Air Force, Uncle Keith and Aunt Hope are having a baby, and Damon has a daughter. I met them both and now Elizabeth is dead. I was scared to think of what could happen next.

'How do I handle all of this by myself?' I was living a double life, full of lies and secrets. But then again, I had been taught to keep secrets all my life. The weight of it all was far too much. I hadn't heard from Carmen or Rodney in years, but I so wished I had them in my life right now.

Jan Davis

CHAPTER 24

How could I tell Damon, Elizabeth was dead? The only thing to do was tell him the truth, but telling him the truth could prove very hazardous to my health. He forbid me to ever bring the subject up again. Even though I was a grown woman, I still longed for my tree and the peace and protection I once felt there.

It had been foggy and raining for a couple of days, so I called to make sure Damon's flight was on time. He always parked his car at the airport so he didn't have to wait to be picked up. His flight was on time, so I figured he would be home in an hour or so.

I got dressed, and prepared a nice meal for him. I set the table using the flowers he'd sent me, hoping he would still be in a good mood. I was in our bedroom dabbing on perfume when I heard him open the door. "There's my Baby," I called as I made my way into the living room.

"There's my girl!" He called back. I was relieved he

was still in a good mood. We embraced and he kissed me passionately. "Let me put my bags up, Baby and I'll be right back for some of this delicious food," he complimented as he headed for the bedroom.

Damon told me all about his business trip and I tried to stay focused, but my mind was on Heather and Elizabeth. All day I tried to find the courage to tell him, but I just couldn't. I was so afraid of how he would react. I couldn't chance setting him off and I certainly couldn't take another violent beating.

After eating, he said he needed to go into the office for a few hours and then run a few errands. I fell asleep on the couch waiting for him to get home. I didn't hear him come in, but he kissed my forehead and woke me. "Hey Honey, you're back."

"Yep, I'm back. I'm going to jump in the shower."

"Alright, good night Honey." I climbed into bed, but sleep was the last thing on my mind. How in the world was I going to handle this? I had to plan a Memorial Service for Elizabeth and be there for Heather. Even though I really didn't know Elizabeth, I grieved her death. She worked so hard to get her life back on track – it all seemed so unfair.

Damon came out of the shower and called my name, but I pretended to be sleep. He got into bed and was snoring within a few minutes. I couldn't turn my mind off. I needed help. In a flash, Aunt Joan came to my mind. *'Perfect!'* I'll call her first thing when I get to work in the morning. She'll help me sort things out…I hope. I finally drifted off to sleep.

I woke to the smell of fresh brewed coffee and the sound of the morning news. Damon was already up, getting ready for work. I was exhausted and could certainly use a cup of coffee. "Good morning, Honey," I greeted trying to sound chipper and refreshed.

"Morn'n."

"How did you sleep?

"Fine, will you please be quiet. I'm trying to watch the news." His good mood was obviously over. I poured myself a cup of coffee and sat at the kitchen table. My thoughts picked up where they left off last night, but Damon broke our silence, "I have to go into work early today, so I gotta get outta here."

"Okay...Are you officially assigned to the Skylar project?"

"Don't know yet, we have an early meeting to discuss it, but I hope not. Whoever gets the assignment will have to travel every week for the next six months or so. I'm afraid the boss will give it to me, since I've already laid the ground work for the project. I have a pretty good relationship with the New York team, but I need to be home, so I can keep an eye on things."

I didn't respond, but was so hoping they would choose him. He grabbed his coat and briefcase and was out the door. I watched as he pulled out the garage, drove to the corner, and turned. I made a mad dash for the phone and called Aunt Joan. I couldn't dial her number fast enough. "Hello."

"Hi Aunt Joan, its Angel, how are you doing? Are

you busy, can you talk a few minutes?" I said in one breath.

"I am well, thank you for asking. Of course I can talk. What's that I hear in your voice?"

"What do you mean?"

"Angel, this old cat can't be fooled by a kitten. Now what's going on sweetheart?"

We talked for an hour and I told her almost everything. I even told her about Uncle Donny and his secrets. I just couldn't tell her about daddy raping me, it would have crushed her. It felt so good to get it all out… well, most of it.

"My goodness, it sounds like a TV movie, and what happened to you, Elizabeth, and that sweet little girl is all so tragic. It was nothing but the grace of God that you're still sane enough put your shoes on the right feet. Now Angel, I know you think you have a beef with God, but the fact of the matter is honey, you desperately need Him. Only He can help you navigate your way through this mess. I know you're angry, but He can handle your anger, and He has never stopped loving you. All I know to do is pray. Will you pray with me Angel?"

The weight of everything drove me to my knees. "Yes, Ma'am, I'll pray with you."

Aunt Joan prayed the most beautiful prayer I had ever heard. I felt an amazing peace as she prayed. A peace I had never known. "Angel, I'm going hang up now and seek the Lord and pray some more. We need His direction. Can we meet for lunch today?"

"Yes Ma'am. I'll just have to think of something to tell Damon."

"Tell Damon, your Aunt Joan is taking you to lunch...period."

"Oh, Aunt Joan, I wish it were that easy."

"It will be that easy today. Now, let me think. The last time I was in your neck of the woods, I stopped at a little restaurant. I think it was called The Breezy something or other."

"Yes Ma'am, The Breezy Grill on Everett Street."

"That's it. If I leave at 9:00am, I should get there by noon. Is that good for you dear?"

"Yes, Ma'am, that's perfect."

"Wonderful. I'll meet you there at noon then."

"Thank you so much Aunt Joan. I'm so sorry to unload on you like this, but I had to talk to somebody."

"Absolutely, no need to apologize my Dear. God knows what we need and when we need it."

"I'll see you at noon Aunt Joan."

"I'll be there."

Noon couldn't come fast enough. I had no idea of what to expect, but I trusted Aunt Joan and I admired her strength.

I made a quick call to the hospital to check on Heather. The nurse said she was still improving, but she constantly asked for her mother. I told her I'd left several messages for the Social Worker, but had not received a return call. She promised she would let the Social Worker know I was trying to reach her.

Damon was in meetings most of the morning, but called me to his office around 10am. "Hello Mrs. Carter, Mr. Carter is expecting you, go right on in," his secretary greeted me warmly.

"Thank you Shelly."

As soon as I opened the door, I could see Damon was upset. "They chose me for the project!"

I tried to keep my composure. I wanted to jump up and down and do a happy dance. "Oh, no Baby. When do you have to leave?"

"I've got to go home and pack a bag now. I gotta be on a plane back to New York at 3:20pm."

"Well, how long will you be gone?"

"I'm not sure. I won't know until I get there and speak with the project managers."

"Is there anything I can do to help?"

"Angel, you listen to me and listen well. I run a tight ship…here and at home. Remembering that, will really be good for your health."

"Of course, Damon. You know how much I respect you. I've learned my lesson."

"I hope so, because if not, I can teach you all over again. You know what I mean?" He cut his eyes at me and I knew exactly what he meant.

"Yes…yes Damon. Don't worry." I walked him to the parking garage, gave him a kiss and promised I would be a good little wife.

I completed a few things at the office before heading to meet Aunt Joan. "Table for two, please."

"Right this way please." I followed the waiter to the table. At noon, on the dot, Aunt Joan walked through the door. I waived to get her attention. When we embraced I wanted to fall to pieces, but somehow pulled strength from her. The waiter, interrupted. "Good afternoon ladies. What will you have to drink?"

"I'll have water with lemon please," I requested.

"Me too, please….thanks."

"Aunt Joan, I have some wonderful news. Damon was chosen for a project that will require him to be out of town for the next six months and he leaves today at 3:15."

"Thank you Lord for answering prayers! We'll deal with him later. In the meantime, I have a dear friend, Tasha Grady, she's the Director for Child Protective Services here in Jefferson City. I've already spoken to her, she's going to look into the case and call me back. Now, tell me again how the sweet baby's mother died."

"The Police Chief said she lost control of her car and ran into oncoming traffic in I44. He said it was a miracle that Heather survived."

"From the things you've told me, Damon was defiant about not having children and quite frankly, he's not a fit father anyway."

"Aunt Joan, when I saw that precious little girl, I instantly fell in love with her. I believe Damon will too."

"Well, the jury's still out on that. Until things are

sorted out, Tasha will make sure she is with a good family when she's released from the hospital."

"Thanks Aunt Joan that would be great, but she's in my heart already. I know Heather is supposed to be with me. I can't tell you how I know, I just know. It's like my momma used to say, "*I just feel it in my spirit.*""

"God is in complete control my Dear. He will work it all out…and I know that in *my* spirit."

"You always know just what to say Aunt Joan, thank you. I have one more obstacle. I have to plan the Memorial Service for Elizabeth."

"How sad. There was no one, but her and Heather? Maybe, you can give the shelter a call. Where was it now? It was a battered women's shelter, right?"

"Yes, Ma'am, It was called *"New Life Shelter."* That's a great idea. I'll give them a call when I get back to the office. I know they would want to be there. Maybe they'll go visit Heather too. She really needs a familiar face right now."

"Now Angel my Dear, let's talk about you. Angel, what I'm going to say is going to be hard for you to swallow, but it needs to be said. I see the same un-forgiveness and bitterness building in your soul that was in John's. Someone once said un-forgiveness is like you drinking poison but expecting someone else to die. I know life has been hard, but your future doesn't have to be a repeat performance of your past."

"Can't you see Angel, it's cyclical. John was abused, he abused Donna, and now Damon is abusing you."

"Aunt Joan, it's not the same. Damon is nothing like

daddy. Yes, I push his buttons and sometimes he loses his temper, but he would never do the things daddy did."

"Angel, it's like ice cream. There's vanilla, strawberry, and butter pecan. There are different flavors, but it's all still ice cream. Abuse is abuse. While Damon is gone, there's something I want you to do for yourself."

"What's that?"

"I want you to come to church with me every Sunday. The only way, and I mean the ONLY way you're going to get through this is with the help of the Lord."

I reluctantly agreed. Aunt Joan had so much wisdom and there was a peace about her that commanded the very atmosphere around her to be at peace as well. I didn't agree with her comparison of Damon to daddy, but I respected her advice.

We talked a bit longer, then I had to get back to the office. I thanked her and told her how much I appreciated her making herself available to me. Before she left she wrote several Scriptures on a napkin gave them to me and made me promise to read them. Again, I agreed.

As soon as I got back to the office, I called the shelter. "Good afternoon, thank you for calling New Life, how may I assist you?" The pleasant voice answered.

"Hello, my name is Angel Carter; may I speak with the Director please?"

"One moment please, let me see if Mrs. Lopez is available."

"Thank you, Ma'am."

"Good afternoon, this is Andrea Lopez, how may I help you?"

"Hello Ms. Lopez, my name is Angel Carter. I am calling in regard to a former resident, Elizabeth Carter."

There was silence on the phone for a few seconds. "Hello?"

"Oh, please forgive me. I...I still can't believe she's gone and poor Heather. Are you related to her? We didn't think she had any living relatives."

"No Ma'am, I'm not directly related to her. I'm married to Damon, Heather's father."

Again, there was silence. "Oh, I see," her tone changed.

"Mrs. Lopez, I had never met or even heard of Elizabeth until just days before she died. She told me she had no living relatives, so I am planning a memorial service for her. She spoke so highly of you and the shelter, I knew you would want to be there. Also, I wanted to ask a favor of you. Would you mind visiting Heather in the hospital? She misses her mother so much and I believe she really needs a familiar face right now."

"Oh, thank you so much." Her tone changed again. "Of course, me and as many of the staff as possible will be there. We loved Elizabeth; she was a wonderful person with a beautiful spirit. My only comfort knowing that she is with the Lord now. I tried several times to visit Heather, but they wouldn't allow me because I wasn't a relative."

"That won't be a problem. We can meet at the hospital and visit her together if you like."

"That would be wonderful Mrs. Carter. I thank you for your kindness and graciousness. I hope I'm not being too forward, but, may I ask how are you doing with Damon?"

"I know you have heard the horror stories concerning Heather and Damon's relationship, but rest assured he loves me. We're fine. People do change you know."

"Forgive me Mrs. Carter, but I'd have to see that to believe it. Is it okay to meet you at the hospital this evening?"

"That's perfect. I'm going after work. So I'll see you there, say, about 6:00?"

"That sounds fine. Mrs. Carter, thank you again. I really do appreciate you allowing me to see Heather."

"Thank you Mrs. Lopez. I'll see you this evening."

When I arrived, Mrs. Lopez was waiting for me. After the usual ID checks, we made our way to Heather's room. "Auntie Andrea!" Heather's eyes lit up as she lunged for Mrs. Lopez.

"Oh, how are you doing my beautiful Mija! Auntie Andrea has missed you so much."

"Auntie Andrea, where's Mommy? I want my Mommy."

Mrs. Lopez looked at me for the okay to tell her. I nodded as tears streamed down my face. I thought it would be much better to hear the terrible news from someone close to her. It was obvious Heather was very fond of Mrs. Lopez. "Well Honey," Mrs. Lopez began, "do you remember the bad car accident you and your mommy were in a few days ago?"

"Yes Ma'am. I hurt my tummy, but I'm all better now."

"That's right. Sweetheart, your mommy got hurt too, only she…she didn't get better. She went to Heaven, Honey. She's with Jesus now."

"I want to go to Heaven too, Auntie Andrea. I want to go with mommy," she said as tears filled eyes.

"Oh Heather," she said embracing her, "I know you do, but it's not time for you to go yet."

"But when can I go?"

"You'll know when it's time Mija, I promise you'll know and I promise you'll see your mommy again one day. I know you miss her, but everyday she's watching you from Heaven. Remember that always, okay."

"Okay, but I still wish I could go to Heaven to see mommy now," Heather wiped her tears.

"Auntie Andrea has a surprise for you." Mrs. Lopez reached in her bag and pulled out a beautiful, cuddly, snow white teddy bear. Heather smiled slightly and thanked her as she embraced the bear, hugging it tightly.

"What a beautiful teddy bear Heather. You play with teddy bear. Mrs. Lopez and I are going to talk with your nurse for just a minute, okay Princess."

"Are you coming back Aunt Angel?"

"Why of course I am Princess. I'll be back in just few minutes."

"Okay," she softly answered.

"Hello, I'm Angel Carter and this is Mrs. Lopez. I'm Heather's step-mother. Is it possible to speak with her doctor?"

"Hi Mrs. Carter, I'm Cindy," she greeted extending her hand. "Dr. Bloom just left her room a few minutes ago so he couldn't have gotten too far. I'll page him for you."

"That's great. Thank you so much."

It was only a few minutes before I was being introduced to Dr. Bloom and shaking his hand. "It's a pleasure to meet you. I'm Angel Cater, Heather's step-mother and this is Mrs. Lopez, a dear friend of her mother's. How is she doing Doctor?"

"Other than missing her mother, she's really doing quite well. She's eating and drinking and using the restroom regularly. We want to keep her here for a few more days to monitor her kidney and liver function, but right now, we're expecting her to make a full recovery. I do have a question for you Mrs. Carter, has anyone told Heather her mother died?"

"As you can imagine, it's been really difficult, but Mrs. Lopez just told her. You see, I just recently met Heather, I thought it would be a better coming from someone she's known and trusted. She cried and of course she really doesn't understand the concept of death. It breaks my heart to see her cry."

"It will take some time Mrs. Carter, but one of the

most fascinating things about kids is their resiliency. I wish we could somehow hang on to that quality as we age. With lots of love, she'll thrive. She's an amazing little girl."

"I whole-heartedly agree. Thank you so much Dr. Bloom, I appreciate your time."

"Yes, thank you for taking such wonderful care of her," Mrs. Lopez replied as she shook Dr. Bloom's hand.

"Absolutely, not a problem. Here's my card, please feel free to call me Mrs. Carter. My nurse will page me and I'll get back to you as soon as I can. It's been a pleasure."

Mrs. Lopez and I played with Heather and her new teddy bear for an hour before reading her a bedtime story. She finally couldn't keep her little eyes open any longer and drifted off to sleep. We both kissed her and tipped out.

CHAPTER 25

On the way home, Damon called to let me know he had made it to New York and was settled in his room. I breathed a sigh of relief that there were several states between us, giving me time to work with Aunt Joan on a solution. One thing was crystal clear; I couldn't do this by myself. I finally realized I needed God.

The next day, I spoke with the Social Worker, Juanita Lacy. She told me that the Director, Tasha Grady, contacted her and she would make sure that Heather was placed with a good foster family and she would allow me and Mrs. Lopez to visit her. I wished she could come home with me, but I knew Aunt Joan was right. Damon wasn't ready and I had no idea if or when he would be.

Later that afternoon, I was in the middle of working on a document for the Executive Director when my cell rang. It was Chief Hammond. "Good afternoon Mrs. Carter."

"Hello Chief Hammond, how are you?"

"I'm well Mrs. Carter, thank you for asking. I promised I would call you after the investigation."

"Yes Sir."

"Mrs. Carter, Elizabeth Hicks lost control of her car because she had no brakes. Her brake line was cut. We're ruling her death as a homicide."

Fear gripped me. "Her brake line was cut…a homicide. I don't understand. Are you saying this was done on purpose…someone murdered her?"

"That's exactly what I'm saying. Mrs. Carter, I will need to speak with your husband. Is he available?"

"No, he's in New York again on business. Why do you need to speak with him?"

"It's routine in any investigation to speak with the people the victim knew. Obviously the circle of people she knew was pretty small. I'm going to need his contact information."

"Yes. Sure…not a problem. He's staying at the Plaza Grand Hotel, in New York. I'm not sure of his room number, but the phone number is 212-555-5500. Chief, my husband doesn't know that I know about Elizabeth's death. I didn't want to upset him. He's been managing a special project at work and he's under a great deal of stress already. Does he have to know that you called and spoke with me?"

"I see. I can't make any promises Mrs. Carter, but I won't volunteer any information."

"Thank you so much, I appreciate it."

"Thank you Mrs. Carter. I'll be in touch."

"You're welcome. Enjoy the rest of your day."

I immediately called Aunt Joan and told her. She simply said, "Angel, everything done in the dark will come to the light."

I explained to her that the Chief said it was just their routine and of course Damon had nothing to do with her death. "Aunt Joan, I know what you are thinking. Damon has his issues, but he's simply not capable of doing something like that. I'm sure of it."

"Well, maybe you're right. At least one of your problems is solved. You don't have to worry about telling him now. I'm quite sure the police will tell him everything."

"Yes, you're right. I asked the detective not to let Damon know that he'd already told me everything. He has this thing about respect. He would be furious. Aunt Joan, I've got to go, Damon is calling me on the other line."

"Okay, Dear. I'll keep praying."

"Me too. Goodbye Aunt Joan."

"Hi Damon, did Chief Hammond call you?"

"You know he did. Why did you give him my information! How stupid can you be?"

"Damon, he's the police, you don't lie to the police. Besides, we have nothing to hide. It's just routine. What kind of horrible monster would do something like that? Did he tell you that the baby survived?"

"Good for her. I told you she's not my kid."

"So what do the police want you to do?"

"They asked me a bunch of stupid questions. I answered them, so it's over. Don't ever give anyone any information about me without asking me first, do you understand me?! This is my business. I swear, sometimes I think it's just air in your head."

"I'm sorry…yes, of course Honey." Even with hundreds of miles between us, I still feared him.

While Damon was in New York, Mrs. Lopez and I planned a small memorial service for Elizabeth. Juanita Lacy, the Social Worker, thought it would be best if Heather attended to help bring some closure and assist in the grieving process. I called and spoke with Dr. Bloom, who immediately agreed and suggested we hold the memorial service in the chapel at the hospital.

Heather sat right between me and Mrs. Lopez. Aunt Joan, Dr. Bloom, Juanita Lacy, several of the nurses and some of the staff from the shelter attended. I held Heather close to my side as the Chaplain gave the eulogy. Mrs. Lopez provided a beautiful picture of Elizabeth for the memorial and I bought flowers. With all I had been through, I had never experienced anything so sad. At least I had my momma until I was just about grown, Elizabeth had no one.

I knew it would take a miracle for Damon to allow Heather to come live with us. After all, he was still denying she was his child. A miracle is exactly what I prayed for. Sunday morning came before I knew it and it was time to keep my promise to Aunt Joan. I didn't know what to expect, but I was determined go.

I pulled up to the church and sat there for a few minutes. I was glad it wasn't a big church, it was small and quaint. Colorful flowers lined the walkway to the steps. There were the traditional stained glass windows, but upon a closer look, it was actually contact paper made to resemble stained glass. Of course, there was the cross that sat prominently on top of the church calling all to come.

Thoughts of New Hope flooded my mind and how much I loved going to church with Momma and Alex when I was a child. Thinking of the songs, the old saints, and the testimony service warmed my heart. So much has happened since then. I had messed up so much and run so very far from God, that I didn't think even He could find me, or would even want to for that matter. But somewhere, deep, deep down in my soul I wanted to be found – I was certainly lost.

I gathered my courage, got out of the car and started up the walk way. "Good morning Sister," a pleasant lady wearing a blue church hat with matching purse and shoes greeted.

"Good morning Ma'am."

After several more good morning's I found a seat in the back. Aunt Joan spotted me and waived, "Come sit up here with me darling." I was hesitant but obeyed and sat next to her on the second pew.

Immediately, those same old thoughts began to bombard my mind. *"Why don't you just give up? Do you honestly think God will forgive you for all you've done? You told Him you hated Him, why would He ever do anything for you? Face it you're just not a lovable person. You're a lost cause. You're filthy."*

"Look at all these church people staring at you. They're judging you Angel. Looking down their church noses at you. You don't have to take this. Just leave. You don't owe anybody anything."

I tried to resist the thoughts and join in the singing. They sang some of the same songs we sang at New Hope, but the words became living to me and somehow began to make their way through the fortress I'd spent years building around my heart.

The louder I sang the more the thoughts began to fade. I could no longer contain myself as I began to weep. I missed Momma so much, but it was more than that. I could feel…I could feel love. I could feel God's love. It was warm and completely satisfying. There was no condemnation. For the first time, as far back as I could remember, there absolutely was no fear. I felt secure and safe. I felt peace. Yes, that was what that feeling was. Peace.

What was I doing? I had to pull myself together. I was not going to fall apart in this little church in front of all these strangers. The sermon, of course, was on the Prodigal Son. God has a sense of humor. The brokenness in my heart battled with his sermon for the entire thirty minutes. I felt like screaming!

Now, the time I dreaded. – The Altar Call. The thoughts were so loud I thought everyone could hear them. *"I know you are not even thinking about going to that Altar. No, you sit right here in this seat where it's safe. You are who and what you are Angel, a nothing, nobody, drug addict and whore. Do you want to be exposed? All your secrets Angel…all your dirty little secrets will come out in the open. Everybody will know just how filthy you are! Everybody will know you're a whore. Don't you dare move!"*

Aunt Joan reached over and took my hand. "Angel, if you want to go, I'll go with you."

I said nothing. I just sat and cried, "Please, let this be over!"

All of a sudden, my legs, without the consent of my brain, began to move. I found myself walking down the aisle to the Altar, with Aunt Joan was right by my side. I stood there, tears streaming down my face, wanting to talk to God, but not knowing where to begin.

I had done so much, failed so many times, so unworthy, so ashamed, so broken and fragmented. How in the world would God begin to put all the pieces back together, would He even want to? I was desolate, a throw away, certainly not usable by God.

I heard Aunt Joan praying for me and I was amazed at how she prayed. I was startled when I felt someone take my hand. I opened my eyes and it was the lady in the blue church hat. She had removed her hat and was ready to war in prayer for my soul. She looked directly into my eyes and began to quote Scriptures. *"Yea, I have loved you with an everlasting love. I rejoice over you with singing, For I know the plans I have for you, thoughts of good and not of evil, to bring you to an expected hope and future, says the Lord."*

With each verse she quoted, the thoughts that once combated every word spoken since the church service began, just dissipated. The power of the spoken Word of God silenced them. I could hear…I could finally clearly hear. I raised my hands and all I could verbalize was,

"I'm sorry. I'm so very, very sorry, Lord. I don't understand how or why You love me, but I am so grateful for your love. It's…it's saving my life. Oh God, why did you leave me?"

For the first time in my life I heard the audible voice of the Most High God. *"Angel, I never left you…you left Me."* His voice was perfectly strong and perfectly gentle at the same time. *"I've never left you. You left me."*

I heard His voice, I felt Him. God had never been so real to me. Nothing changed in my situation that day, but absolutely everything changed in my spirit and soul. God came for me that day. He didn't send His angles, He came for me Himself, for that, I am forever grateful.

CHAPTER 26

J uanita Lacy, Heather's Social Worker, suggested Heather be allowed to stay with Mrs. Lopez when she was released from the hospital until the final arrangements were made. What a God idea and I couldn't thank Him enough. At the time it was the best place for her. She needed to have some connection to her mother.

Heather and I had grown very close over a short period of time. The nurses said she would even ask for me during the day. I didn't know whether it was because she missed her mom or not, but I was grateful for it.

God had given me the courage to tell Uncle Keith, Aunt Hope, and Alex that Damon had a daughter and about Elizabeth's death. I also told them about how God moved for me at church with Aunt Joan. With Damon gone for another two weeks, I asked Uncle Keith and Aunt Hope to come to visit for the weekend. I wanted them to meet Heather. I also called Aunt Joan and asked if she would come, they all agreed.

When we arrived at the hospital, I asked them to let me talk to Heather first. I wanted to let her know I had brought some very special people I would like her to meet.

"Hi Heather."

"Aunt Angel!" She stretched out her arms for a hug.

I grabbed her and held her tight. "How is my little Princess today? I have a surprise for you. I brought some very special people I want you to meet. Is that okay?"

"Uh huh," she nodded.

Aunt Hope looked at me and said, "She's absolutely precious."

We visited and played games with her until it was nap time. I held her, sang her to sleep and gave her a soft kiss on those chubby little cheeks of hers and we quietly left. As we made our way to the elevators, with tears in her eyes, Aunt Hope asked, "Angel, what's going to happen to her?"

"Aunt Joan explained that she spoke to her friend and arranged for her to be placed with Mrs. Lopez and we could visit her there until everything was sorted out."

"I don't know Angel, Damon was pretty adamant about not having children. Is he open to the idea of her coming to live you with the two you?"

"No, not at all. It's going to take a move of God, Aunt Hope."

"Amen to that," Aunt Joan agreed, "but God is able."

"Yes He is, but He won't override Damon's will," Uncle Keith commented.

"Oh, but God has a way. He'll either say yes to God or God will simply move him out of the way. You know the old saying, *'One monkey don't stop no show.'*" Aunt Joan has such a way with words.

"Aunt Hope, I trust God to somehow work it all out."

"It's so good to hear you say that Angel. You're absolutely right, He will."

"Thanks Aunt Hope. It won't be long before you and Uncle Keith will be bringing home your own little bundle of joy."

"That's right, just three and a half more months and I can't wait!" Uncle Keith said proudly as he rubbed her belly.

"Oh no, Aunt Hope, with all this craziness going on, we haven't even talked about your baby shower."

"Oh my goodness, you're right Angel," Aunt Joan agreed we've got to get busy."

"Ha, I forgot about it myself," Aunt Hope chuckled.

I enjoyed my time with them so much. The fellowship was so sweet. I didn't realize how much work and energy it took to hold on to bitterness and un-forgiveness. I was so free. Did I still have issues... absolutely, but the issues no longer had me.

We left the hospital and went back to my house since Damon wasn't there. I was in my room freshening up, getting ready to take everyone to dinner when the doorbell rang. "Uncle Keith, will you answer the door please?" I yelled from my bedroom.

"Sure."

"Hello Sir, I'm Sergeant Samuel Jacobs with the Jefferson County Police Department. Is Mr. Damon Carter here?"

"Hello Sir, I'm Keith. Damon is away on business. What's this about?"

"I just needed to ask him a few questions. Is his wife…" he took the note pad from his pocket, flipped few pages and glanced at the name, "Angel Carter available?"

"Yes, come in. I'll get her for you."

Uncle Keith knocked on my bedroom door. "Angel, there is a police officer here looking for Damon, he needs to speak with you."

My heart started racing. "Okay, Uncle Keith, I'll be right out." I hurried to put my shoes on and walked into the living room.

"Hello, I'm Angel Carter, Damon's wife. My Uncle tells me that you were looking for Damon," I extended my hand.

"Yes Ma'am. Just need to ask him a few questions. May I speak to you in private?"

"No need for that, this is my family, you can speak freely in front of them. What's going on Sergeant?"

"Quite frankly Mrs. Carter, your husband is a person of interest in the murder of Elizabeth Hicks."

My knees buckled, but Uncle Keith caught me. "I'm

sure there's some mistake. My husband isn't that kind of man."

Uncle Keith helped me to the sofa. "Ma'am, we simply want to ask him a few more questions," the Sergeant assured.

"Sergeant Jacobs, may I speak with you outside please?" Uncle Keith requested.

"Yes, absolutely." Uncle Keith grabbed his jacket. Twenty minutes later, he came back in.

I heard Sergeant Jacobs' car pulling off and jumped to my feet. "What did he say Uncle Keith? What's going on?"

"Angel, I need you to tell me the truth. Does Damon hit you?"

"No, of course not," I lied. "What are they talking about, Uncle Keith?" I was defensive.

Aunt Joan looked at me, she knew I was lying, but didn't say a word. "It seems that when Damon and Elizabeth lived together, he abused her frequently. So much so, that she left him in the middle of the night while he slept and she and Heather checked into a battered woman's shelter. She lived there for an entire year. Mrs. Lopez said she stayed to herself, but she worked hard to get back on her feet," Uncle Keith informed the room.

"When the investigation found the brake lines on Elizabeth's car had been intentionally cut, her death was ruled a homicide. Now the investigation has been turned over to Sergeant Jacobs," he continued.

"With no siblings and both parents deceased, they

had very little information as to who would want to harm her. That's until they discovered Damon had just been ordered to pay $2,500.00 a month in child support."

Aunt Hope looked stunned, "Angel?! So, are they trying to implicate Damon in her murder?" she asked surprised.

"That may be the case. But right now, they just want to talk to him," Uncle Keith answered.

Again, my knees got weak. "Damon is arrogant, egotistic and a jerk, but I don't believe he's capable of murder," Aunt Hope commented.

"You're right Aunt Hope; he's definitely not capable of murder. I admit, he's not perfect but, he's not really a jerk either, you just haven't gotten to know him.

"Well, Jacobs got a call while we were talking. He was told that his office had spoken to Damon and he told them he would be home Monday to answer all of their questions. Don't worry Angel. They have to question everyone, it's their job."

Uncle Keith was always the voice of reason. "You're right, let's go eat. It will all be fine."

Before we left, I called Damon, but got his voice mail. I left him a message to call me.

CHAPTER 27

Damon finally called late Sunday night after everyone left. "Damon I've been worried out of my mind about you. Why didn't you call?"

"Why were you worried? You knew where I was. I was working."

"What about the police, Damon? They said you told them you were coming home tomorrow to go down to the precinct to answer their questions."

"Yes, I did, and I will. No big deal. I'll be home tomorrow evening."

I was amazed at how calm he was. So much so, that I believed him. It was no big deal. He would simply answer their questions and that would be that. "Damon, what about Heather?" I asked.

"I'm going to tell you for the last time. She's not my child!"

"But Damon the..."

"No more questions! Why are you questioning me

like you're the police? Why do you continue to disrespect me Angel? I've got to go."

"I miss you. I'll see you tomorrow, Baby." Without saying another word, he hung up.

I called to let the family know he was alright and would be home tomorrow. I tried to stay focused at work, but my mind kept going back to Heather and Damon. I couldn't concentrate, so I left early.

Even though I knew in my heart Heather was his daughter, I had to settle it in my mind. So, I went to the Bureau of Vital Statistics to try to get a copy of Heather's birth certificate. I figured, since I was her step-mother it wouldn't be a problem. I was right! I paid the $12 fee and the lady handed me the envelope. I got in the car and ripped it open. I couldn't read fast enough. Not only did it list Damon Carter as the father, he had even signed it.

"How many more lies!!!" I wanted to confront him and tell him all his lies had been exposed. But fear and the memory of the beatings brought my sanity back so instead, I found myself wanting to make sure there was a nice home cooked meal waiting for him when he got back.

I stopped at the market and got everything I needed to prepare his favorite meal. As I turned the corner there were police cars everywhere. I couldn't even pull into my driveway. I parked a few doors down and quickly walked toward our house. An officer stopped me before I could get any closer. "Officer, what's going on? That's my house."

"Are you Angel Carter?"

"Yes, what is all this!"

"Please come with me. The Sergeant wants to see you."

I ran in the door and there were police everywhere, looking through everything. "Sergeant, what's going on, what are you doing here?"

"Mrs. Carter, I have a warrant to search your premises."

"Search?! What on earth or you looking for?!"

"Please, sit down Mrs. Carter." I quickly tried to find a seat out of their way.

"Long story short, the person that tampered with Elizabeth Hicks brake line left several foot prints in the mud next to her driveway. We lifted those prints and had them sent to the lab."

"I'm sorry Sergeant. I'm trying to follow you, but what does any of that have to do with Damon and me?"

"The footprints we lifted were very unique, Mrs. Carter." Just then, one of the officers called him to the bedroom. "Please excuse me Mrs. Carter."

I was so nervous, I couldn't control my trembling. A few minutes later he came back with a bag in his hand. "As I was saying Mrs. Carter; the footprints were unique. They were boots with a pattern on the bottom...a cobra."

The boots I saw under the bed! The brown boots with the cobra imprint on the bottom – Damon's boots.

"Sergeant, there has to be some explanation. Surely more than one pair of those boots was sold."

"No doubt, but it looks pretty incriminating when your husband has a pair that matches the size and wear pattern of the foot prints we found at the scene of the crime. Not to mention the dried mud found on them. Mrs. Carter, it's enough evidence to charge him with the murder of Elizabeth Hicks."

I sat there in shock. *'Damon, a murderer.'*

"Okay everyone. Let's pack it up. We found what we were looking for. Mrs. Carter, you seem like a really nice lady. I'm sorry it had to come to this. He will be arrested at the airport as soon as he steps off the plane."

I called Uncle Keith and told him they were charging Damon with murder. He immediately drove back to the house to pick me up. "There is no way I'm going to leave you here Angel. Damon is wanted for murder. You're coming to stay with us where you'll be safe."

On the way back to Uncle Keith's house, Sergeant Jacobs called. "Mrs. Carter, your husband was not on the plane. He checked in for the flight, but never actually boarded the plane. Have you spoken to him? And Mrs. Carter, remember, you can be charged with aiding a fugitive if you don't tell us the truth."

"Yes, he did call me last night, but he said he would be home this evening and he was going to answer all of your questions. He didn't tell me what time the flight arrived. He always parks at the airport, so I don't have to pick him up. I have no idea where he is."

"Don't worry, wherever he is, we'll find him."

My head was spinning. How could I have been so blind? What about Heather? The drive back to Uncle Keith's house was a blur. I must have called Damon's cell phone a hundred times. We arrived at the house and I passed out from sheer emotional and physical exhaustion.

The sun creeping though the window woke me and I jumped up and ran into the kitchen. Uncle Keith and Aunt Hope were drinking coffee talking about all the craziness going on. "Oh, Angel, I'm so very sorry about all of this. Don't worry you're safe here with us," Aunt Hope consoled.

"I have so many questions. I feel so stupid. I should have listened to you both. Uncle Keith, I lied. Damon has been abusing me."

"What?! Why would you lie Angel? Why would you take his abuse? You knew I was here for you." Uncle Keith looked confused as tears filled his eyes. "All I can say is, I hope they catch him before I do!"

"That's exactly why I didn't tell you Uncle Keith. I knew how you would react and I couldn't chance you ruining your career. You've worked too hard. I couldn't drag you into my madness."

"Baby, it's all water under the bridge now. Angel is here safe with us. I know you're upset, but she's been through enough," Aunt Hope tried to calm Uncle Keith. "Now listen, I have a doctor's appointment, we'll only be gone a few hours. You can come with us."

"Thank you Aunt Hope, but I just want try to relax and have a hot cup of coffee."

"Okay, we shouldn't be gone more than a few hours. Please call us as soon as you hear something Angel."

"I will Uncle Keith. Listen, I can't thank you both enough for loving me. As bad as things are, I feel much better being here with you both."

They left for the doctor's office and I poured myself a cup of coffee, turned on the TV and sat down on the sofa. After a few minutes I dozed off. "I knew you would run to your family and betray me."

I opened my eyes and Damon was standing over me. I tried to jump up, but he held me down. "You have been nothing but disrespectful and ungrateful since I married you. You're a piece of trash, just like my mother was."

"Damon, no!!! I loved you and I tried so hard to show you."

"You defied me. You disrespected me. You betrayed me. You lied to me." His voice was low and his fist was clinched. I covered my face, bracing for the first blow. But it wouldn't be his fist this time, he pulled out a gun.

"Damon!!! What are you doing, Honey. I'm so sorry!!! I promise I'll never do it again. I love you. Don't do this please, please!!!"

"You're such a liar. All you women are liars!!! He yelled. "I told her I didn't want kids, but she defied me too. She got pregnant on purpose, and then wanted to make me pay for her choice to have that kid. I told her to have an abortion, but she wouldn't listen to me. Disrespectful! But I made sure she wouldn't get a dime."

"Damon, no…what did you do?!" I cried.

He stared off into nowhere as he began his sick story. "I hated her for what she did to me. I tried to talk some sense to her, but she wouldn't listen, just like you."

"I took a later flight to New York that day. I went to her house and tried to talk to her, to reason with her, but she didn't even have the decency to open the door... after all I've done for her. Her car was parked in the driveway. It was so easy. I just got cable cutters out of my toolbox in the trunk of my car and simply cut her break line. She deserved to die!!! You all deserve to die!!!"

Damon turned his attention back to me and hit me in my face with the barrel of the gun. I heard my jaw crack as I fell to the floor. He kicked me several times, and then pulled me to the bedroom by my hair. I could feel my hair being pulled out by its roots. I was begging him to stop. He picked me up and threw me onto the bed. I tried to run again, but he pulled me back. I tried to fight back, but it made the rage worse. He hit me in my stomach and again I fell to the floor where he stomped my head, I passed out.

The excruciating pain coursing through my body demanded I regain conciseness, but I could hardly move. Where was he? How long had I been out? I didn't know if it was safe to try to get up or not. What time was it? I didn't want Uncle Keith and Aunt Hope to walk in. I knew he wouldn't hesitate to kill them both.

I struggled to get on my feet, but had to settle for crawling. The house was a mess. My blood was everywhere. Furniture was turned upside down. There was broken glass; drawers had been emptied onto the couch and floor. I was confused. What's happening? Damon was nowhere to be found.

Frantically, I searched for my cell phone. I needed help, I was in bad shape. I crawled toward the door trying to avoid the shards of glass. I stopped suddenly in my tracks. Maybe Damon thought I was dead, so he tried to make it look like someone broke in and beat me to death. Or maybe he knew I wasn't dead and was coming back to finish what he had started.

I had to reach the top lock, but every part of my being was in intense pain. After several attempts, I finally got it unlocked and crawled outside screaming through the pain of my broken jaw. A few neighbors start opening their doors to see what all the commotion was about. "Please help me!!! Please!!!"

Suddenly, I heard the garage door opening. I knew Damon was just yards away. He was waiting for Uncle Keith and Aunt Hope. He screamed and cursed at their neighbors, telling them to mind their own business and then pulled the gun out and they all backed up.

"This is all your fault, you know. We could have been happy if you would have just respected me and obeyed me. Now look at what you've done."

Damon aimed the gun directly at my head. I closed my eyes and told myself it would all be over soon. Then I thought, *'What will happen to Heather.'* Suddenly, somewhere deep in my heart, God awakened my will to live. I was badly beaten, but I prayed for strength.

God answered, and with my right foot I kicked him as hard as I could. He lost his balance and the gun went off. He and the gun fell to the ground...I was shot. Several men jumped on Damon and kept him pinned on the ground until the police arrived.

I lay there, just a few feet from him, bleeding. "Oh God...how did I get here?" Feeling the blood rushing from my body, it felt strangely warm against my cold skin. *Is this it? Is this the end?* I thought, hearing the sirens in the distance. *'Are they coming for me?'*

How did all this happen? How could I have let this happen? Where was I when my life began to spiral out of control? What was I thinking? "Lord, please help me. Please..."

That's my tragic story. The sirens were coming for me and Damon. He would spend the rest of his life in prison. I remembered Elizabeth begging me, saying, "Angel, don't stay too long. I remembered the day I saw that lady testifying in church die. I remembered how very peaceful it was and how I had seen her beautiful Angelic escort. I waited for my Angelic escort.

We both lay on the cold ground awaiting our fates, our eyes met and I whispered, "I forgive you." He cursed and turned his head.

CHAPTER 28

I regained consciousness three days later at City General Hospital in the Intensive Care Unit. *'Where was I? What happened?'* I panicked. I couldn't speak and my head was pounding. I was confused and began thrashing about. Two nurses rushed to my side, one tried to calm me while the other called the doctor.

"It's okay Angel, it's okay. You're safe now. You're at City General Hospital. We're taking good care of you. We're going to get the doctor in here to talk with you in just a bit. I just want you to relax. Do you need something for pain?"

"Yes," I nodded. Tears filled my eyes as the awful memory of all that had happened began to overtake me. "Heather, where's Heather?" I tried to speak but couldn't open my mouth.

"Your jaw was broken, Angel. Let me get you a pen and paper so you can write. Can you manage with your finger in the splint?"

Again, I nodded, "yes."

As I began to write, the doctor walked in. WHERE IS HEATHER?

"Hi Angel, I'm Dr. Lee. Who is Heather?"

MY STEP-DAUGHTER. IS MY FAMILY OKAY? DO THEY KNOW I'M HERE?

"Yes, Angel they do. I have spoken to them every day since you arrived. As a matter of fact, the nurses tell me that you've had many visitors."

DID MY FAMILY SAY ANYTHING ABOUT HEATHER?

"I'm sure Heather is just fine. You've got to focus on getting better. You've been through quite an ordeal Angel. You were severely beaten, but you're going to be okay. You've had surgery to reset your broken jaw and finger. Your jaw had to be wired so the bone can heal properly. It usually takes about four to six weeks to heal, and then we'll remove the wire."

"Until then, it's a liquid diet. You were shot in your right side, but the bullet missed your vital organs and we were able to remove it with no complications. You also had a concussion and two broken ribs. You're a very lucky lady, Angel."

I knew luck had absolutely nothing to do with it. "I'm sure your family will be here soon." Dr. Lee continued. "Until then, what I need you to do is rest. I'll have the nurses give you something for pain and to help you rest."

I CAN'T REST UNTIL I KNOW WHERE HEATHER IS!!!

"Cassie, will you please call her family and let them know she's asking for them?" He instructed.

"Yes Dr. Lee."

"Angel, one of the nurses will be in to give some medicine for the pain and to help you relax. You need both, doctor's orders," he smiled, patted me on the hand, then he and the other nurse excused themselves. A few minutes later, Cassie came in and injected medicine into my IV and I was out like a light.

I could hear someone calling my name. Struggling to open my eyes and gain focus, the most beautiful sight finally came into view. Uncle Keith, Aunt Hope, Alex, Aunt Joan and Sister Johnson were smiling with tears in their eyes. I motioned for the control to raise the bed and pointed to the pen and pad to communicate. "Thank you Jesus!" A very pregnant Aunt Hope proclaimed, followed by Sister Johnson's "Praise the Lord! Baby, it's so good to see you with your eyes open."

"You talk about praying. Sweetness, we've been praying 'round the clock for you and God in His love and mercy has answered," Sister Johnson rejoiced.

I LOVE YOU ALL SO MUCH! WHERE IS HEATHER?

"Don't worry Angel, she's doing wonderful. She's been asking for you, but I assured her you would be there to see her just as soon as you could," Uncle Keith assured.

I was so relieved. I MISS HER SO MUCH. BUT OF COURSE, SHE CAN'T SEE ME LIKE THIS. I MUST LOOK HORRIBLE.

"She misses you too, Princess. You'll see her soon, don't worry. When you're ready, I'll bring her to see you myself."

THANK YOU UNCLE KEITH. I'M SO VERY SORRY ABOUT YOUR HOUSE. I'LL PAY FOR ALL THE REPAIRS AND REPLACE EVERYTHING HE DESTROYED.

"Angel that should be the furthest thing from your mind, because it's the furthest thing from ours. We are all just so thankful that you're gonna be okay," Aunt Hope said.

WHAT'S GOING TO HAPPEN TO DAMON?

"They charged him with the murder of Elizabeth and your attempted murder. Because of the brutality of his crimes, the judge refused bail. He'll probably never see the free world again. Angel, I've had to do my share of forgiving, but this was a really hard one. I had some very ungodly thoughts for a while. It's a good thing for him that they denied bail. I'll never, ever, let anyone hurt you again Angel," Alex said vehemently.

YOU'RE AN INCREDIBLE BROTHER ALEX. ABSOULTELY NONE OF THIS IS YOUR FAULT. I'VE MADE POOR CHOICES.

"Now, you've got to focus on getting better so you can get out of here. I know that hand of yours must be tired from all that writing. We're going to let you get some rest. If you need anything, I mean anything at all;

don't hesitate to give me a call. Everyone at church told me to tell you "hello" and they're praying for you too."

THANKS AUNT JOAN. THANK YOU ALL FOR LOVING ME. I'VE MADE SO MANY STUPID MISTAKES. PLEASE FORGIVE ME FOR NOT LISTENING TO YOU.

"Well join the club, Honey. Every single one of us has been a card carrying member of that club, at one time or another, Precious. Your past is your past. As long as you leave the past in the past and don't go try'n' to drag it into your future, you'll be fine. God is a healer. He heals us inside and out." Aunt Joan had such wisdom and I adored her for it. They kissed me on my forehead before leaving. It wasn't long before I drifted off.

Since Aunt Joan worked at the hospital, she popped in to see me several times a day. I enjoyed her visits. One day she came in with huge grin on her face.

HI AUNT JOAN. YOU LOOK LIKE THE CAT THAT SWOLLOWED THE CANARY. WHAT'S GOING ON?

"We'll my Dear; I was talking to Dr. Lee about your progress, which by the way is amazing. When I mentioned your name, one of the other doctors overheard. I believe you may know him.

NO MA'AM, I'M AFRAID NOT. HE MUST BE MISTAKEN. I DON'T KNOW ANY DOCTORS PERSONALLY.

Well, he's right outside your door. Maybe if you see him, it will jog your memory. "Doctor, please come on in."

She opened the door and I couldn't believe my eyes. It was Rodney Walker...Dr. Rodney Walker in the flesh! "Hi Angel, I am so very, very happy to see you."

DOCTOR??? WOW!

"Yep, it's been a lot of hard work, and still is, but it's been worth it. Angel, I'm so very sorry for all that you've been through. It's so wonderful to see you again after all these years."

IT'S GREAT TO SEE YOU TOO! YOU WERE SUCH A GREAT FRIEND. I NEVER GOT THE CHANCE TO THANK YOU FOR THAT. THANK YOU!

"The pleasure has been mine Angel. This time, I'm not losing touch. I promise."

GOOD, I'D LIKE THAT.

I spent three weeks in the hospital, then six weeks in therapy. I had a lot of time to pray, study the Scriptures, and assess my life. I was determined to make some changes. I was determined to walk in forgiveness and allow God to heal me; both inside and out. I was determined to surrender my life, my heart, my all to the Lord, and asked that He work in me. I confessed my forgiveness for daddy, Uncle Donny, Damon, and all the others that abused and mishandled me. The hardest person to forgive was...me.

CHAPTER 29

TWO YEARS LATER...

The transformation is amazing. The pain and trauma I suffered was no longer my master. With the help of the Lord, I made it my servant. I had a testimony and it was my mandate to share it with others.

Damon and I were divorced, and I moved on with my life, but I prayed for him. I understand all too well the damage abuse and un-forgiveness can do. But it is God's will that none perish, but all come into repentance, so I pray for him every day.

The courts gave me full custody of Heather and I adopted her. I can't begin to describe the joy she brings me. She loves school and can already read. It's been a transition for her too, but with love and nurturing, her resilience is amazing. She also has starting to call me "Mommy." The first time was absolute music to my ears.

I made great money at Baker Technologies, but resigned after going back to school and earning my Christian Counseling Certification. In six months, I'll open the "Donna - Elizabeth New Chapter Women's Shelter" right here in Jefferson City. The name is a bit lengthy, but I wanted to honor Momma and Elizabeth. Both were very brave women that I will always admire.

My heart is filled with such gratitude and joy. God made a choice of me, I *get* to do ministry. I was a throw-away, but God came for me. He gave me beauty for ashes and the oil of joy for mourning.

Alex is an extraordinary young man. He has already been promoted to Master Sergeant in the Air Force. He's stationed in California and has his eye on a young lady at his church. I can't wait to meet her.

My Cousin Joshua, Uncle Keith and Aunt Hope's son is simply wonderful. He's so cute and growing like a weed. Of course, they couldn't be prouder. He and Heather are great playmates. Aunt Hope's Father and birth Mother are typical grandparents, they love spoiling Joshua and Heather too.

Sister Johnson's mother passed. She was ninety four and lived a rich full life. She says her mother is probably having deep theological discussions with Moses, Elijah, and Paul in Heaven. She moved back to Springfield, she and Aunt Joan have become the best of friends.

And then, there's Dr. Rodney Walker. What can I say; he's been in my heart since elementary school. He is such a godly, honorable man and so patient with me. He's teaching me how a man should treat a woman. The level of respect I have for him is tremendous. He's naturally great with Heather after working with kids for years.

What my journey has taught me is that unforgiveness will eat you like cancer. Hatred will erode and decay your heart, even self–hatred. The walls we build around our hearts to protect ourselves, quickly become your very own, self-made prison. While they may protect us to some degree, they keep out the forgiveness and healing we so desperately need from God.

I've learned that there are just some things we may never understand, God is sovereign but He doesn't waste anything. Every time I counsel a young woman, I know exactly how she feels. I've walked in her shoes and I know there is hope and healing on the other side of her pain. I've learned that my abusers were also very broken. Their brokenness just manifested in a different manner. It's kinda like ice cream; there are different flavors, but still ice cream.

I don't want to mislead you, the transformation hasn't been easy and there are times I've felt like giving up. But God would send an encouraging word through Rodney or a gentle kiss on the cheek from Heather and my determination would be renewed. There were times I had to put on my big girl panties and encourage myself and I'd find that God's amazing Grace was always more than enough.

No matter who you are, what you've done, or what's

been done to you, God loves you and wants to heal you too. He absolutely has a plan for your life. There is help, healing, and wholeness for you in Jesus.

EPILOGUE...

Today the "Donna - Elizabeth New Chapter Women's Shelter" opened and a beautiful young lady walked in. "Good morning, my name is Angel Sanders. How may I serve you today?"

"Umm, I have a friend whose boyfriend is hitting her. My friend lives with him because I...I mean she, just found out she's pregnant. Her mother put her out and she doesn't know what to do."

"Tell your '*friend*' that we would love to help her," I smiled. Let me show you around our home so you can tell her all about it."

Relieved, she smiled, "Yes Ma'am, I'd like that."